Also by J.A. Lang

Chef Maurice and the Wrath of Grapes (Book 2)
Chef Maurice and the Bunny-Boiler Bake off (Book 3)

CHEF MAURICE
AND A SPOT OF TRUFFLE

J.A. Lang

PURPLE
PANDA
PRESS

Paperback edition published by Purple Panda Press

ISBN 978 1 910679 02 9

To Mum

PROLOGUE

It had not been a good day. Hamilton knew about good days, and this was not one of them. First there'd been that rude early morning awakening, the sky still dark outside, and a bumpy car ride out into the middle of nowhere.

Then came a long walk through endless unfamiliar woods, the only bright spot being the mud—oh, how he loved a good patch of mud—to a clearing surrounded by tangled trees. Finally, a rope loosely tied to his collar, a convenient tree stump, and then they disappeared back the way they came. Forever.

The sun was high before he managed to wriggle his way free, and close to setting by the time he stumbled across a pitted dirt track leading, presumably, to somewhere better than nowhere.

A veering car, screeching tyres, a man jumping out, shouting, "Crikey, is that one of those—" And then a large cardboard box, rough but kind hands, and Hamilton was trapped. Again.

1

Now he sat in his cell, picking at the evening's meagre dinner, listening to his nearby cellmates yowl and snap and whimper.

It was a dog's life; it really was. No, scrap that.

A dog's life would have been *better*.

CHAPTER 1

Chef Maurice, proprietor and head chef of Le Cochon Rouge, Beakley, was facing a problem of mushrooming proportion.

He stood in the walk-in fridge, hands thrust upon hips. They were all gone. The chanterelles, the cèpes, the oysters, even the humble white button—not a mushroom in sight.

"Where are all my *champignons?*" he demanded, striding back into the kitchens.

Patrick, his sous-chef, looked up from behind a half-peeled pile of carrots and glanced at the wall calendar.

"Ollie should have been by now, chef. Want me to give him a call?"

Ollie was the village's resident wild food importer and local forager, rooting through the Cotswold countryside to turn up edible flowers, herbs and leafy greens and, come autumn, picking his way through the medley of wild mushrooms that sprung silently in the nearby woodlands.

"Bah," said Chef Maurice. "*Probablement*, he has found the woods empty and is ashamed to put his face at our door."

He strode over to the kitchen's back entrance, stuck his head out and sniffed the morning air, his large moustache aquiver. Autumn in Beakley was turning out unseasonably warm thus far, and the leaves were still undecided as to whether to shed their summer hues. But even so, the recent heavy downpours should have heralded a plentiful crop of mushrooms this week.

"*Mais non*, the weather, it is correct. It is impossible that he has found no mushrooms! So why does he not come?"

"I bumped into him down in the village the other day," said Patrick, peeling away industriously. "He seemed pretty chuffed about something."

Chef Maurice frowned. A happy supplier was not necessarily a good thing. For years he'd had the pick of Ollie's foraged findings, but recently the capital's haute cuisine brigade had cottoned on to the riches of the English countryside—no doubt encouraged by how the word 'wild' prefacing any ingredient now made it doubly desirable in the eyes of their diners—and Chef Maurice had found himself outbid for Ollie's produce on more than one occasion.

As owner of Beakley village's one and only restaurant, he felt that Ollie should have at least displayed him a little neighbourly consideration—ideally in the form of a generous discount—but the local forager was apparently a firm believer in free market forces.

"Oh, and he mentioned he might have something new for our menu too," added Patrick.

"New?"

That was enough. The chance to berate his mushroom supplier about the late delivery and recent price hikes, coupled with the possibility of snagging a new ingredient for the day's menu, was incentive enough to propel Chef Maurice out of the door and down into the village, where Ollie rented half a cottage on the southern outskirts.

He rang the doorbell, then, no response forthcoming, ambled round to the back. Chefs were generally more comfortable with back doors, anyhow; the front was for guests, the postman, and the forcible ejection of unruly customers who, for some unfathomable reason, had yet to grasp the concept that the chef is always right.

At least in the case when the chef in question was Chef Maurice.

He rapped on the back door, which creaked open at his touch. Glancing down, he took in the splintered mess where the lock had been and the door knob now dangling awkwardly off one screw.

"'Allo?"

He nudged the door open with his boot. It swung inwards halfway, stopped by a pile of assorted muddy footwear. Chef Maurice sucked in his stomach and squeezed himself through.

They say one should never trust a thin chef. By this measure, Chef Maurice was very trustworthy indeed.

"'Allo?" he called again. No reply. He turned to go, but then a thought gave him a nudge. Seeing as he was here . . .

Ollie's kitchen was a mess of old dried plants and the crusted remains of microwave meals. Chef Maurice tut-tutted and made his way over to the large double fridge—refrigeration being a key tool in the mushroom supply business.

Et voilà! Lined up neatly inside the fridge were several plastic boxes, each with the name of a restaurant scrawled on the side.

Chef Maurice pulled out the one labelled *Le Cochon Rogue*—he rather liked how the misspelling lent the name a somewhat rakish air—and lifted the mesh lid. It wasn't quite full, but at least Ollie had managed a decent selection; a handful of fat cèpes, a generous pile of hedgehog mushrooms (so called because of their soft, spiky undersides), a bag of little white puffballs, and a sizeable chunk of chicken-of-the-woods (a thick, fleshy mushroom and one of Chef Maurice's favourites).

He had a peek into the other boxes, to check that no rival had secured a better selection. Thus engrossed, he didn't notice the shadowy figure creeping up behind him until it hit him hard across the head.

CHAPTER 2

Chef Maurice spun around with a yelp and ended up with a face full of feather duster.

"Thief!" crowed Mrs Eldridge, who lived next door in the other half of the cottage and had the sort of countenance that brought to mind that of a particularly aggrieved turkey. She prodded him in the stomach with the duster. "I saw you, don't deny it!"

"Thief? Do I have the look of a thief?" Chef Maurice drew himself up and puffed out his chest.

A slim figure with a neat blond ponytail appeared in the doorway.

"Right, what's going on here?"

It was PC Lucy Gavistone, of the Cowton and Beakley Constabulary, and the only member of the force who lived in Beakley itself. She ate at Le Cochon Rouge every Sunday lunch and always tipped well.

"Ah, Mademoiselle Lucy! Let me explain—"

"I saw 'im! Breaking in the back like a common criminal—"

"That is a lie! The door, it was already broken."

"So you thought you'd just help yourself, eh? These foreigners, think they can just waltz in and take anything they—"

PC Lucy held up a hand. "That's enough, both of you. Mrs Eldridge, I'm sure Mr Manchot had no intention of theft in mind. Don't worry about the door, Mr Manchot, Ollie already reported the break-in last Friday. I told him to get that lock fixed sooner than later."

"I had to make him call 'em, you know," said Mrs Eldridge, nudging Chef Maurice. "Just like 'im to not want to call, but I said what happens if they took something valuable?"

"But they did not?"

"Not a thing, he said."

Chef Maurice shook his head at the ineptitude of burglars these days.

PC Lucy pulled out her notebook. "Mrs Eldridge, you said on the phone just now that you haven't seen Ollie for a few days?"

"Not since Saturday morning, I haven't. He went off early as usual, and I ain't heard a peep from him since."

"And he has failed today to make his weekly delivery," added Chef Maurice, turning back to the fridge.

PC Lucy scribbled this down. "Well, it's Monday now, so that's only two days so far. Ollie knows his way around the woods, I doubt anything serious has happened to him. But if he doesn't turn up in the next few days—"

She broke off at the sight of the large box in Chef Maurice's arms.

"It is my delivery," he said. "I simply come to collect it."

"See, told you," said Mrs Eldridge smugly.

PC Lucy looked unimpressed. "Unless you have written permission from Mr Meadows, I'm afraid I can't let you take anything away from the property—"

"But they will spoil!" The tone of his voice suggested this was a crime worse than murder.

"Then we better hope that Ollie turns up soon. In the meantime . . . " She pointed meaningfully towards the fridge.

Reluctantly, he placed the box back inside and shut the door.

Never mind, he thought as PC Lucy shooed him and Mrs Eldridge back out the way they had come. There was always Mushroom Liberation Plan B.

A late evening breeze ruffled the leaves overhead. Arthur Wordington-Smythe drew a deep breath of the cool night air and sighed in satisfaction. Autumn in Beakley didn't get much better than this.

By his side, Horace, his Great Dane—or to be more accurate, Meryl's—padded along, nose hanging to the ground, occasionally looking up at Arthur with an expression of doleful reproach.

These postprandial walks had been Meryl's idea, a chance for her two favourite males to bond, she'd said.

Arthur, however, had suspicions that this new evening regime had been precipitated by the newfangled exercise videos Meryl had found down at the library—the type that required leg warmers, copious amounts of buttock-waggling, and a skinny lady in a leotard and headset yelling encouragements about the size of your thighs.

Up until this point, Arthur had never paid much attention to the state of his thighs. If pressed, he'd have had to concede that they did a jolly good job keeping his knees and hips attached to one another, though nowadays his right hamstring was giving him the occasional twinge on a cold winter's night.

He'd said as much to Meryl, perhaps in rather too strident a tone, as these mandatory strolls had been instituted very soon after.

Horace, who was now reaching an age where nothing but a big bowl of bone marrow and liver could move him from his oversized basket, looked up at Arthur again and rolled his eyes.

Nevertheless, Arthur was in a good mood. He'd returned from London having experienced lunch at a restaurant so epically ill-conceived that the review would practically write itself. The readers of the England Observer were particularly partial to the well-placed metaphorical boot when it came to food criticism; the greater the vitriol—masked, of course, in the arch and the urbane—the more they lapped it up. And Arthur, their long-standing restaurant critic, was more than happy to oblige.

It wasn't as if the reviews were utterly undeserved. Some places, especially those temples to glitzy fashion and expense-account-fuelled eating that sprang up every year in Central London, like toadstools after the rains, positively begged to be taken down a peg or two—or, at least, down a padded hanger with an engraved coat-check number. But today's lunch had been a disaster of quite a different ilk . . .

Just off Hoxton Square, occupying the ground floor of a converted warehouse, he'd made his first (and no doubt last) encounter with Soil, the recently launched down-to-earth endeavour of Marcus Motley, previously best known for his short-lived fish restaurant, the baldly named Sea.

That review had been quite the corker too. It turned out that most diners were unaccountably squeamish about tucking into their pan-fried sea bream when surrounded by a giant circular aquarium filled with its staring brethren, while the sharkskin seating had turned out to have a particularly abrasive quality that ruined more than a few Savile Row suits before being swiftly removed (the seating, that is, not the suits).

Now there was Soil. Taking the recent trend in locavore-ism to the next level, Motley's latest venue only served ingredients foraged from within a five-mile radius of the restaurant. All rather admirable, except for one problem: the only wild food growing within a five-mile radius of Hoxton appeared to be about fifteen different types of weed that all tasted like parsley.

As for local game, one just had to take a look at the nearby feral pigeon population to immediately turn vegetarian for the duration of dinner.

Arthur paused under a handy street lamp to rummage in his pockets for a pen and notebook. Horace took the opportunity to sniff out the latest canine gossip, then lifted one arthritic leg to add his own comment.

They were now down past the end of the village, where the street lamp budget had petered out. A movement in the shadows back up the street, near the end cottages, caught Arthur's attention.

Tugging on Horace's lead—Horace harrumphing as they went—Arthur inched forwards to get a closer look. There had been something about the way the shadow had moved . . .

As they neared the building closest to them, the left half of which belonged to old Mrs Eldridge, Arthur saw a tall figure, slim and clothed in black, slip around the far side of the cottage, the half that was rented by that forager fellow, Ollie Meadows. There was the sound of a door creaking open and closed, but no scrape of a key and, odder still, no lights came on inside.

Arthur considered his options. There was a small possibility that Ollie had just come home—young people these days kept all kinds of hours—and possessed excellent night vision plus the frugal desire to reduce his electricity bills. On the other hand . . .

He glanced down at Horace who, given the short pause,

had taken the opportunity to lie down in the middle of the road and had started to snore.

No, Horace would be of little use if it came to confronting an opportunistic burglar. Better to—

Another indistinct form, prowling in the shadows, was approaching the cottage from the direction of the village. Except this second figure was of significantly more robust proportions, and wore a white jacket and dark checked trousers. Moonlight glinted off steel-capped boots.

The figure turned its head this way and that, and for a moment Arthur caught sight of a very large, very familiar moustache.

What in the devil—

"Maurice!" hissed Arthur, but his friend was too far away. Soon, the chef had crabbed his way around to the back of the cottage and disappeared too.

Arthur broke into a run, or at least what his knees declared to be a run at this point in life. Horace, waking up with a grunt, pulled himself to his paws and lolloped along after his master.

They were halfway to the cottage when they heard an almighty crash and a muffled cry.

"Maurice!" shouted Arthur.

CHAPTER 3

The door banged open and a dark figure sprinted away over the back fields.

"Maurice!" shouted Arthur again, urging his knees onwards. As he neared the cottage, he could hear an increasingly disgruntled stream of inventive French swear words. He slowed his pace; no one with that command and volume of language could be severely injured.

He eventually located his friend in the kitchen, pinned down by a large upturned oak table. The floor was covered in dried plants, mushrooms and a handful of shrivelled apples. Arthur bent down gingerly, making certain to straighten his back, and heaved on one corner of the table. Chef Maurice scrambled out, still swearing heatedly.

"He came from nowhere! I walk in here, and boom"— he slapped his hands—"the table tips and I am trapped! *Quel désastre!*"

"Whoever he was, he was in here before you," said Arthur, and quickly related what he had witnessed. "My question is—and do understand I probably don't want to

14

hear the answer but feel it necessary to ask anyhow—why are *you* here?"

Chef Maurice stuck out his chest. "I have come to collect my mushroom delivery. I already have come today, but the police lady, she would not allow me to take them."

"So you thought it'd be a good idea to break in and steal them?"

"Steal?" Chef Maurice looked momentarily shocked. "*Mon ami*, I do not steal. I will of course pay Monsieur Ollie. When he appears again, of course."

"Appears?" This did not sound good.

"He has not been seen since the Saturday," said Chef Maurice, and proceeded with what Arthur presumed to be a rather sensationalised retelling of his morning adventures. "I tell Mademoiselle Lucy, it is *criminel* for him to miss a delivery like this!"

Arthur watched as the chef stooped down and started scooping fallen mushrooms into a handy paper bag.

"You do realise you're disturbing a potential crime scene?"

"Bah, I would not have the need to disturb if the intruder had not attacked me with the table. I will simply liberate these delicious *champignons* to make use of before they go bad."

"But why would anyone—apart from a nut like you, Maurice—want to break in here?" Arthur thought about what his friend had said about the broken lock. "Twice, even, assuming Friday's break-in was the same person?"

Chef Maurice nodded. "That seems correct. Yet it is most strange that nothing was taken."

Arthur wandered into the cottage's other ground-floor room, a study-cum-living-room littered with books on plants and herbs, as well as partially labelled dried specimens and scraps of paper with scrawled notes and drawings.

He found Horace attempting to take a nap in a battered dog basket four times too small for him.

Nothing looked particularly valuable, although it was hard to tell amongst all this—

"Aha! *Regarde, mon ami!*" shouted a voice from the kitchen.

Arthur hurried back through to find Chef Maurice with his head wedged into the bottom of the fridge.

"There was a certain smell when I was here before," he said, voice muffled by the fridge's contents, "and this nose, it never lies!" In his hand, he waved what looked like a small lumpy potato.

"Um. Very good." Arthur wondered how one was meant to test for concussion, and, more importantly, how to avoid explaining to the doctor exactly how one's friend had come to be hit on the head by someone else's kitchen table.

"Now, Maurice," he said carefully, "put down that potato and let's—"

"Potato?" Chef Maurice backed out of the fridge and gave the lump an appreciative sniff. "This is no potato! *Regarde.*"

Arthur opened his mouth to suggest rapid medical

treatment, but stopped. A familiar, alluring, pungently earthy yet not unpleasant scent filled the air.

"Wait a minute, is that . . . a . . . "

Chef Maurice gently scratched the surface of the lump and the wafting aroma got stronger. "You are correct, *mon ami*. If I am not mistaken, this is a very good, and very expensive, white Alba truffle. And look!"

He pulled a rough sack out of the fridge and held it open. Inside was a heap of fat, pristine white truffles. Altogether, they must have been worth tens of thousands of pounds.

Arthur had a bad feeling about this. But feelings could be dealt with later, once they got out of here.

First, he had to get Chef Maurice to let go of the sack of truffles.

Back in the moonlit kitchens of Le Cochon Rouge, Chef Maurice brushed the last specks of soil off his newly acquired prize, with all the love and care of an archaeologist in a hitherto undiscovered royal tomb.

It was only a single truffle, Arthur having forcibly restrained him from 'liberating' more than one sample, but it was a beauty, nonetheless. He lined a small wooden crate with straw, tucked the truffle in and surrounded it with eggs to keep it company.

Balancing on an upturned bucket, he placed the box reverentially onto the highest shelf in the walk-in fridge, then went to bed.

Perhaps if he'd known just how much trouble these truffles were going to cause in the very near future, he might not have drifted off so easily.

But as things were, sleep engulfed him like autumn fog the minute his head hit the pillow.

That night, he dreamed of truffles.

Hamilton was dreaming too. But his was not a good dream.

In the silence of his cell, his sleep-propelled legs kicked uselessly against the straw and shredded paper that littered the concrete floor.

It was a nightmare about bacon.

Again.

CHAPTER 4

The next morning, Patrick and Alf, Le Cochon Rouge's gangly commis chef, arrived at work to find Chef Maurice bustling round the kitchens, humming to himself.

"Everything all right, chef?" said Patrick. His boss was not, by any definition, a morning person. In fact, there were probably sloths deep in the Amazon jungle that could be considered more morning people than Chef Maurice. That said, sloths weren't generally known for indulging in a large glass of cognac most evenings, which presumably helped their morning routine.

"Everything is very right. *Voilà, regarde ça!*" He held up a straw-lined box, filled with eggs and a lumpy beige object. "Which of you can tell me what this is?"

"Er. A potato?" said Alf, scratching his ear.

Patrick leaned in closer. It looked a lot like a dusty potato, true, but there was something about the smell . . .

"That's not . . . an Alba truffle, is it?" Patrick had only seen one once, during a short stint at one of Paris's top restaurants, and even then it hadn't been as big as this one.

They cost more than . . . well, more than he and Alf were getting paid, that was for certain.

"*Très bien.*" Chef Maurice picked up the truffle and waved it under his nose like a glass of single malt whisky. "And so, this morning, we will enjoy *une belle omelette aux truffes*! That is, after I can find the truffle grater . . . "

As Chef Maurice conducted a whirlwind search around the kitchen, banging open cupboards and drawers and cursing loudly to the God of Lost Kitchen Implements, Alf sidled up to Patrick.

"I thought truffles were made of chocolate," said the commis chef, out of the corner of his mouth. "How come chef wants to make a chocolate omelette?"

"It's not a chocolate truffle, Alf. It's a *truffle* truffle."

Alf looked up at him blankly. Patrick sought another approach.

"It's a type of mushroom. It grows underground."

"So . . . like a potato, then?"

"No! Not like a potato. They grow on the roots of trees, it's a sort of symbiotic relationship. They work together," he added, seeing Alf's forehead wrinkle. "The tree and the truffle."

"Aaah, gotcha. So how come chef's all excited about a mushroom?"

There was the sound of tumbling boxes from deep inside the storeroom.

"Well, for one thing, they're really expensive," said Patrick. "A truffle like that, from Alba—that's in the north in Italy—can fetch up to a couple of thousand pounds per kilo, you know. They call it the King of Truffles."

"Bah!" shouted an indistinct voice from the storeroom. "The white truffles of Alba, they cannot compare to the black truffle of Périgord. *La truffe noire*, she is the Queen of Truffles! The texture, the aromas . . . "

"Black truffles cost less, though," said Patrick to Alf. He raised his voice. "So you're saying a queen is better than a king, chef?"

"*Absolument!*" Chef Maurice was a feminist, it seemed, at least when it came to truffles. "Aha! Now we can begin." He emerged triumphantly, waving a small metal slicer.

"So, these truffles," said Alf, as if trying out a new idea. "These expensive truffles. They just grow in the ground, yeah, like, in the woods?"

"If only," said Patrick. "We don't get this type around here in England. We only get the cheaper types, like summer truffles, and even then they're nearly impossible to find."

"Bah," said Chef Maurice, "the English truffle. It is like the English wine. It cannot compare! Now, observe."

He slid the truffle across the grater. Thin, almost translucent slivers fell to the plate, beigy-brown marbled by a network of thin white veins. An intense aroma of forest floor mixed with garlic drifted through the kitchen.

"So are we thinking of doing a truffle menu, chef?" said Patrick, picking up a slice and holding it up to the light.

"Eh?" Chef Maurice looked up from his slicing. "*Non, non*, this truffle is . . . a sample. From a supplier."

"Ollie's started dealing in truffles?" Patrick was surprised. Ollie was perennially strapped for cash, as he was wont to tell anyone he met. Brokering truffles was far beyond his usual cash flow capabilities.

"*Non, non*, a new supplier," said Chef Maurice hastily. "But enough questions. Now we eat!"

He threw a large knob of butter into a pan, cracked half a dozen eggs into a bowl, and a minute later the three chefs stood around the table in silent anticipation, forks in hand, admiring a perfectly made wobbly omelette topped with slivers of the finest white truffle.

They dove in.

"But if we *did* have these truffles around these parts," said Alf a while later, not being one to let a good idea go, "you mean anyone could just go around and pick them up?"

"It's not that easy," said Patrick. "You can't see them from above ground. You need a special truffle dog, one that's trained to sniff them out from under the earth. In fact, I heard in France they still use pigs to hunt truffles."

"Pah, you do not want a pig," said Chef Maurice, mouth full of truffled omelette. "They are big trouble. Always, it is better to have a dog."

"How come, chef?" asked Alf.

Chef Maurice held up a finger. "With a dog, you can train the dog to give you the truffle after he has found it. With a pig, the pig also wants to eat the truffle. And you do not want to fight a pig for a truffle. I know truffle hunters who have lost more than one finger to a pig who is mad for truffles."

Patrick tried to clear his mind of the mental image of Chef Maurice wrestling a pig for a truffle.

Chef Maurice held the truffle to his nose again, a thoughtful look on his face. Their impromptu breakfast had barely made a dent in it.

"So you're definitely sure we don't have these truffles here in Beakley?" said Alf, running a finger around the plate, then licking it.

Patrick expected some form of emphatic denial from his boss, perhaps along with some slur on the incapacity of England's green and pleasant lands to produce a worthwhile crop of truffles. Instead, Chef Maurice murmured, "It does not appear to be so . . . "

The head chef stared into the distance for a moment, then shook his head.

"*Bon*," he said, slapping the table. "Enough of talk, today we make a terrine of pork with the spiced Bramley apple chutney—Patrick, you know the recipe—and Alf, potatoes and the usual *mélange* of vegetables for the ox cheek stew. We will put it on tonight's menu. *Allez-y!*"

He picked up the rest of the truffle, wrapped it carefully in his handkerchief and pocketed it.

"Now, I must go see a man about a dog."

Patrick tilted his head to one side. There was something about the smell still lingering in the air, and the way his boss had said it . . .

"Not a pig, chef?"

Chef Maurice gave him a long look. "*Non*. A dog, Patrick. Definitely a dog."

PC Lucy Gavistone surveyed the crime scene with a grim look on her face. She was hoping this gave her a look of stern authority, something she felt she sorely lacked in her dealings with the residents of Beakley.

That was the problem with policing in a small village. It wasn't that the residents of Beakley didn't respect the law; they had great respect for it, and therefore liked to turn up en masse to make sure it got done properly.

Hence the ragtag audience currently following her as she made her way round Ollie Meadows' cottage. Okay, she could deal with Arthur Wordington-Smythe, who lived up the top of the village and had been the one to report last night's break-in. Unfortunately he hadn't seen much, just an intruder dressed in dark clothes, tall and thin, most likely male.

This ruled out the possibility of the intruder having been one of her other two spectators.

She wasn't too sure why Chef Maurice, who ran Le Cochon Rouge up at the top of Beakley, was also here. He'd dropped by—as if dropping by a police investigation was a normal morning activity—wanting to speak to Arthur about Arthur's dog, or something along those lines, then had been distracted by the mess in Ollie's kitchen.

She'd have turfed him out if she could, on the grounds

of obstructing the course of justice in general, and that of PC Lucy in particular, but that would have meant also getting rid of old Mrs Eldridge from next door, who was immovable to the crowbars of unsubtle hints and pointed suggestions.

Mrs Eldridge was currently rummaging through the drawers in Ollie's desk, "looking for those clue things," as she put it. PC Lucy felt the need to point out that burglars hardly left their calling cards when they made their rounds.

Unfortunately, burglars were also meant to take things, and this was the second time someone had been here at Ollie's, apparently to do nothing more than stroll around and perhaps make themselves a cup of tea. This vexed her. This wasn't how things were meant to go.

"If only I'd been here last night," sighed Mrs Eldridge. "Of all the nights to go over to Ethel's—her back's playing up again, poor dear—when I could have been here, apprehending criminals and whatnot. Makes you question fate, it does . . . "

No, kicking Mrs Eldridge out at this point would only cause an almighty fuss; plus manhandling members of the public, especially those old enough to be your granny, was generally frowned upon in the force.

"Hmm, now this is rather odd," said Arthur, who was also standing by Ollie's desk. Like much of the rest of the house, it was covered in bits of dried leaves and twigs and was sticky to the touch.

"What's odd?" She followed Arthur's gaze to the large corkboard above the desk. It was bare, apart from a wide rectangular patch of lighter-coloured cork where something had been pinned up.

And torn down. Recently, too.

The four remaining pins each held a corner scrap of paper, grubby and curled at the edges. The many holes in each piece suggested that whatever had been pinned there had been taken down and put back up with some regularity.

She carefully removed the pin from the yellowed scrap nearest to her.

" . . . Civil Parish of Farnl . . . 1957 . . . " she read.

"There was a map there," volunteered Mrs Eldridge. "One of those maps with geography on it, fields and woods and things. It was old, too. Told Ollie he shouldn't be drawing on a nice old map like that."

"Do you think it was valuable?" said Arthur to PC Lucy.

"Perhaps. Though Ollie doesn't strike me as the map-collecting type." PC Lucy dropped the scrap, along with the other three corners, into a plastic bag and sealed it.

"Was the map here after the first break-in?" asked Arthur.

"Oh, yes," said Mrs Eldridge, before PC Lucy could reply. "I'd have noticed a thing like that, I would."

"Plus, Ollie didn't report anything missing. And I'm pretty sure he'd have noticed this"—PC Lucy waved at the bright empty rectangle of cork—"if it hadn't been there then."

There was a loud *thunk* from inside the kitchen, followed by swearing and the sound of several objects thumping and rolling to the ground.

When PC Lucy got there, Chef Maurice was shuffling around on his knees, picking up grubby-looking potatoes and stuffing them into a sack.

"I told you, Mr Manchot, that it is imperative that you do not remove any items from a crime scene!" She looked at the sack. "And they're just potatoes, for goodness' sake. Surely you have bags of them up at the restaurant."

Was it her imagination, or did Chef Maurice and Arthur exchange an odd look at that point?

"So put them back where you found them, and if you're going to be here, at least stick with the rest of us."

Chef Maurice reluctantly opened the fridge and placed the sack inside, muttering something unflattering about policemen and their lack of appreciation for cuisine that wasn't round and filled with jam.

PC Lucy headed upstairs, where a quick tour produced a vignette of life as the common-variety bachelor, all piles of unwashed socks and rumpled linen, though a half-used tube of lipstick and some eyeshadow in the bathroom cupboard suggested that Ollie did manage the occasional bout of female company. In fact, word round the village was that the forager was something of a ladies' man, though so far not a single lady (unattached or otherwise) had been willing to come forward to corroborate this statement.

Chef Maurice tutted at the state of the youth today, while Mrs Eldridge used her walking cane to examine a particularly large pile of laundry.

"You never know who might be hiding in there," she explained.

In the bedroom, unaired and musty, with overtones of muddy boots, PC Lucy gave the room a brisk once-over while her audience stood at the door, offering a range of helpful suggestions, which she dutifully ignored.

At the back of the wardrobe, she discovered Ollie's idea of sound monetary practice: a brown envelope stuffed with just over two thousand pounds in small notes. Not bad for a man constantly complaining about being on the brink of financial ruin. Some of the clothes hanging above looked suspiciously new too.

She hunkered down near the bed and had a brief look under—nothing but dust bunnies and an old empty suit-case—then started picking through the litter bin.

"Ooo, I was just going to suggest that," said Mrs Eldridge.

Bingo. The first crumpled note bore a message in neat bold capitals. The spectators crowded into the room.

"'Keep away from things that don't belong to you. Or else'," read Arthur over her shoulder. "Charming."

Mrs Eldridge was now poking her cane into Ollie's wardrobe, while Chef Maurice settled himself into the old armchair in the corner.

"There's another." PC Lucy smoothed out the second

piece of paper. The writing was thinner, more scrawled, but the message no less threatening.

HAVE COME TO COLLECT MY LOAN. DON'T GIVE ME ANY MORE LIES IF YOU KNOW WHAT'S GOOD FOR YOU.

"Do you reckon they're from the same person?" asked Arthur.

"I don't know. It's not the same handwriting, or at least someone's tried to make it look that way. But don't worry, I'll get to the bottom of it," said PC Lucy, straightening up. She gave the room another sweeping gaze, pondering her next move.

Things weren't looking so good for Ollie. She might have believed he'd done a runner, probably from someone he owed money to, if it wasn't for the big wodge of cash he'd left in his wardrobe. But if he hadn't taken off of his own accord . . .

"Okay, I think that's that. I'll take these notes down to the station. Mrs Eldridge, I'll need a statement from you about the last time you saw Mr Meadows."

She ushered Mrs Eldridge down to the living room, while taking a moment to head off Chef Maurice, who was trying to sneak into the kitchen again.

"Have a good morning, gentlemen," she said, as she led him and Arthur firmly out the back door. "Oh, and try not to tell the whole of Beakley about what you saw today, okay? The Cowton and Beakley Constabulary are more than capable of finding Mr Meadows. If he is, in fact, missing."

It was unfortunate that Ollie wasn't particularly popular down at the station, what with all the trouble he caused when he periodically got caught foraging on private land. Reporting him missing after a few days would probably cause looks of relief rather than consternation.

She thought about the two notes now in her pocket. Despite what she'd just told Arthur and Chef Maurice, she had her doubts as to whether the police would be able to find Ollie—especially if someone, given the content of those notes, didn't want him to be found.

She walked back into the cottage, a sudden chill running down her back.

CHAPTER 5

Back at the Wordington-Smythe house, Arthur filled the kettle and turned on the stove. "You really should have told the police about the truffles."

"I did. I showed them to her," said Chef Maurice, inspecting the contents of the biscuit tin and selecting a home-made jammy dodger. "If she thinks they are potatoes, then what is there for me to do?" He gave an expansive shrug.

"Well, for a start, you could have told her that there are thousands of pounds' worth of white truffles sitting in the fridge of a property that's now been burgled twice in the last four days."

"Bah," said Chef Maurice, waving his biscuit. "If the thief did not find them, he did not want to find them. And we know it is for the map that he came, *non*? You said that yourself."

Arthur poured them each a cup of Earl Grey tea, which Chef Maurice accepted with a little sniff. After several decades in the country, he'd finally given in to the thoroughly British enjoyment of a 'nice cuppa', though he still insisted on his mandatory three sugar cubes.

"I *said* the map is definitely an item of interest. But whoever it was might have been after the truffles too."

"Then why do they not take them?"

"Oh, I don't know," replied Arthur, dunking a biscuit in his tea. "Maybe he was disturbed by the screaming Frenchman trapped under a solid plank of oak."

"I did not scream," said Chef Maurice, calmly picking out a second jammy dodger. "And it was not my fault. It was he who pushed the table on me."

Arthur drummed his fingers on the table. "I still don't understand this map business. If it was in any way valuable, why rip it off the wall like that? The house was empty. He could have taken out the pins and rolled it up, not grabbed it like a child in a playpen."

"Perhaps not all thieves are so exact as you, *mon ami*."

"So it appears."

There was a grunt from beneath the kitchen table. Arthur retrieved a bone-shaped biscuit from the second, much larger tin and tossed it under the table. There was a slobbering gulp followed by a happy rumble.

"So what did you want to borrow Horace for, anyway?"

"Aha," said Chef Maurice, waggling his eyebrows. He fished around in his pocket until he found the handkerchief, which he unwrapped with care. "Smell this."

Arthur took a long deep breath. "Magnificent," he murmured. "Alba, isn't it?" He picked up the truffle and studied the cut surface.

"That is exactly what I ponder. They say the *arôme* of a truffle comes not just from the variety, but from the tree itself that it grows with. Many years ago, I have been to Alba, seen the trees, eaten the truffles—"

"Amazed there's any left, then."

"—and though this truffle is similar, my nose smells something different. A little difference, that is true, but there is something there. This truffle, *mon ami*, it smells of the *English* woods."

Arthur gave the truffle another sniff. "I thought no one's been able to cultivate white Alba truffles anywhere, let alone here in England. I'm certain I'd have heard if any had been found growing in these parts."

"But would you? Those who deal in truffles, they have very closed lips. These truffles, they may be closer than we think."

Arthur paused, then slapped both hands on the table. "The map! Of course! Maurice, suppose Ollie actually found those truffles near here, and he marked his patch on that map. Mrs Eldridge said something about him drawing all over it. Just think—"

"I already have. And I have come to the same thought. These truffles, there is a chance they come not from Italy, but from much nearer here. But without a map, we must find them by ourselves. *Donc*, the need for your *chien*."

Horace lifted his head and gave them both a sleepy-eyed look.

"You think Horace here can sniff out truffles?"

"With the necessary training. Which we must do fast. Do not forget, if the map shows the way to the truffles, we are not the only ones looking. And the other person, they now have the advantage of directions."

He waved the truffle under Horace's big wet nose. "Horace, *allons-y*! We go to find truffles!"

Horace blinked, rolled his head to the other side of his basket, and started to snore.

They say you can't teach an old dog new tricks.

Arthur wished that this principle also applied to Chef Maurice, every time he came up with another of his hare-brained schemes.

Horace had so far been unmoved by the scented hand-kerchief shoved under his nose. So, with great reluctance, Chef Maurice had carved off a sliver of truffle, placed it on a dog biscuit, and offered up this canine canapé for Horace's inspection.

Horace appeared to enjoy this gourmet treat just fine, and now his breath smelt of Great Dane mixed with Base Notes of Forest Floor. Unfortunately, he still could not be persuaded to get up and follow them into the garden for the next step in the Maurice Manchot Truffle Dog Programme.

"Out of interest, what was the next step going to be?" asked Arthur, as he made them another cup of tea.

"I bury small pieces of truffle around the garden, and Horace, he digs them up."

"Given the number of bones he's already buried and lost out there, I wouldn't give that idea much hope, old chap. It's no good. You're just going to have to find another dog."

He'd expected Chef Maurice to throw in the towel at this point. His friend was not, to put it lightly, an animal person. When pressed by, say, a young child to name his favourite animal, his usual reply was 'Beef'.

But Arthur had underestimated the lure of *la grande mystique*, as the French referred to the mysterious draw of the truffle.

Chef Maurice bent down and offered Horace one last truffle-covered biscuit. Horace shuffled round and placed a paw over his nose. Message: I'm out.

"Very well," said Chef Maurice, standing up and brushing himself off. "We must find another *chien*. Perhaps one"—he threw a glance at Horace—"of a slightly younger vintage."

It was a pleasant, sunny drive over to the Helping Paws Pet Sanctuary in Cowton, the nearest decent-sized town to Beakley. The sky was clear and open, the leaves were slowly turning russet, and the local pheasants were too busy hiding from game hunters to bother running out in front of Chef Maurice's car.

Still, Arthur was not entirely happy with this turn of events.

"Maurice, you do understand that a dog is for life, not just for truffle hunting?"

Chef Maurice turned around in his seat, a hurt look on his face. "*Mon ami*, I assure you, any *chien* who comes into my home will be treated like fam—"

Horns blared as a truck, bearing down on them from the opposite direction, swerved at the last minute to avoid Chef Maurice's little red Citroën.

"Eyes on the road, please," said Arthur, after he'd caught his breath and released his knuckles from their death grip on the side of the car.

"Me and my truffle dog, we will form a team *formidable*. You will see. We will work day and night to find the most delicious truffles. There will be a Cochon Rouge autumn truffle menu." Chef Maurice sighed. "It will be *superbe*."

The Helping Paws Pet Sanctuary was a low-slung brick building on the outskirts of Cowton, surrounded by unkempt fields.

Cheery, if slightly desperate, posters lined the windows, reminding visitors that dogs, cats, budgies, guinea pigs, rabbits and all other small furry friends were for life, not just for Christmas.

By the look of the busy pens inside, it seemed that some people hadn't got the memo.

They pushed open the front door.

"Can I help you?" A spotty-faced youth, wearing a T-shirt proclaiming him 'Barking Mad for Beagles', appeared from around a corner, carrying a large bucket of dried dog food.

Chef Maurice waved his bulging handkerchief. "I am in search of a dog who enjoys the scent of truffles." A thought appeared to occur to him, and he lowered his voice. "Do not tell anyone I said that. This is a secret, *comprends?*"

The youth looked disapprovingly at him. "Chocolate is extremely bad for dogs. It gives them heart trouble." He looked Chef Maurice up and down. "Have you had a dog before? Done any training?"

Chef Maurice looked at Arthur. "Does training a commis chef count?"

"No, commis chefs don't count."

"*Non*, I have not trained a dog before."

"Okay. Well, we do have—"

"But I am not looking for a pet."

"No?"

"I look for a *collègue*. For the hunting of truffles." Chef Maurice slapped his forehead. "Forget that I said that, too."

"O-*kay*." The youth picked up his bucket and started to back away. "I think you'd better speak to my manager . . . " He hurried back the way he came.

Arthur and Chef Maurice sauntered down the row of kennel enclosures. A few ears pricked up, a few noses essayed tentative sniffs at the handkerchief, but none of the candidates seemed sufficiently interested to pass the preliminary interview stage.

They turned left into the Cattery section.

"I have always liked cats," said Chef Maurice.

"You have?"

"They keep themselves clean. They value the beauty of sleep." Chef Maurice ticked an imaginary list off his fingers. "They can climb high walls. And they are suspicious. This is a good thing. *Les chiens*, they are too trusting."

A long-haired Siamese opened her eyes and blinked at them haughtily.

"Sadly," said Chef Maurice, as he waved the handkerchief past the dozen or so lounging cats, "it appears they do not have the interest in truffles."

Down the end of the hallway, they found themselves passing the Miscellaneous Mammals enclosure.

A pair of lop-eared rabbits wrinkled their noses at them curiously, and an extremely fat guinea pig waddled over for a closer look at the visitors.

Arthur peered into the ferret house, which may have looked empty, but certainly didn't smell it.

"Egbert went off to his forever home last week," said a female voice behind him. It belonged to a middle-aged lady in a green jumper, corduroys and sensible brown wellingtons. A plastic name badge introduced her as Tara.

"I'm so sorry to hear that," said Arthur, taking off his hat.

She gave him a strange look. "I meant, he was adopted."

"Oh. Well, er, good for Egbert, then."

"For us too, frankly. He'd been with us for over four months, and I'm afraid it's true what they say. Ferrets really do smell. Can't help it, the poor things."

Arthur nodded. He recalled a distant aunt who'd developed a ferret habit later in life. Relatives would visit with their pockets stuffed with potpourri and take frequent breaks to go outside and admire 'what you've done with the garden'.

"So how can I help today? Looking to bring a ray of sunshine into your happy home?" She smiled at Chef Maurice, who was hunkered down next to what appeared to be an empty pen.

"We— I mean, my friend down there is looking for a dog," said Arthur.

Tara clapped her hands together. "Splendid. Well, if you'd just like to follow me . . . " She bounced away down the hallway.

"Come on then, Maurice."

There was no answer.

Arthur looked back. Chef Maurice was in the process of poking his handkerchief through the wire fencing.

"What are you doing?"

The chef seemed to be engaged in a staring contest with the pen's current resident, who was sitting in the far corner.

"Ah, that's our little Hamilton," said Tara, coming up behind them. "He gets a lot of interest, bless him, but so far no one's quite taken the next step. They need quite a bit of outdoor space, you know."

"Is it me, or is he a bit on the small side?"

"Oh, he's a teacup variety. A micro breed, at least, that's how they're sold. Problem is, people think they're adorable when they're all cute and tiny, but then they get a bit older and some owners get a bit of a shock. They can grow to the size of an adult Labrador. Hamilton here is only a year old, we think. We don't know too much about him, I'm afraid. Someone found him wandering around near the main ring road and brought him in. His collar said Hamilton, so we stuck with the name."

There was a squeaky grunt and Hamilton ran over and grabbed the handkerchief from Chef Maurice's fingers. He trotted around in little circles, snorting happily, then sat down and tried to make a bed out of it.

Chef Maurice looked up, as if noticing Arthur for the first time. "I think," he said, beaming, "that I have found my truffle dog."

"It's a pig, Maurice. A micro-pig."

"Then, I have found my truffle pig!"

In his pen, Hamilton stuck his nose into the handkerchief and took a deep breath.

This was what heaven smelt like.

CHAPTER 6

With the pig-adoption paperwork duly filed, and Tara reassured that Chef Maurice, despite his professional tendencies, had no intention whatsoever of eating Hamilton, they departed the Helping Paws Pet Sanctuary with the little pig perched on Arthur's lap, along with a new dog bed, a large bag of sow nuts—'Pigs Go Nuts For It!' claimed the cheery slogan—and a stack of leaflets on the care and feeding of teacup pigs.

"Washbasin pig, more like it," said Arthur, shifting Hamilton to his other knee. "You're a heavy little fellow, you know that?"

Hamilton, still holding Chef Maurice's handkerchief in his snout, gave Arthur a hurt look that said he was merely big-boned, thank you very much.

That afternoon, Chef Maurice sent Alf out into Le Cochon Rouge's rather overgrown vegetable garden to set up fences and clear the ground for Hamilton's new home.

He prepared himself a late lunch of fresh pasta with grated truffle and parmesan, then picked up a knife and carefully cut several small chunks off the remaining truffle. These he buried all around Hamilton's enclosure, while Dorothy, long-time head waitress and self-declared mother hen of Le Cochon Rouge, took Hamilton off for a much-needed bath.

All pink and scrubbed, Hamilton passed the truffle-detection test with flying colours, sniffing out every single piece Chef Maurice had hidden, as well as unearthing a few onions left over from last winter, an empty bottle of cognac ("How did this get here?" asked Chef Maurice, puzzled) and the spare keys to the shed.

Then it was early dinner—sow nuts for Hamilton, ox cheek stew for the kitchen crew—dinner service, then early to bed for all.

Arthur had donated Horace's old kennel to serve as Hamilton's new outdoor bedroom. Chef Maurice left his newly acquired truffle partner dozing happily next to a bowl of water and a small pile of sow nuts.

Time to get some rest, as tomorrow was going to be a busy day. Quite how busy, though, Chef Maurice had yet to find out.

A low fire crackled in the hearth, the only light source in the shadow-filled room. Two high-backed chairs faced the fireplace, at an angle suggesting that their occupants were rather more interested in the flames than each other's faces.

A heated discussion was well underway.

"—said I'm sorry, how was I meant to know someone else would be—"

"You were *meant* to use your brain. What little of it there is left."

"I'd never have had to be there in the first place if you hadn't gone and sh—"

"You think this is *my* fault? After all your nasty habits and greedy little friends—"

"Fine. Fine! Look, we got what we wanted—"

"And then lost it!" The second voice was older, sourer.

"I'll get it back. I know where to go—"

"After all the rain last night? No." The second voice slammed down like a heavy trapdoor in a gale. "Leave it. You've caused enough trouble as it is."

"Fine. Have it your way." The first voice sounded petulant. And a little relieved. "When do you reckon they'll find … it?"

"How would I know? All I know is"—there was a grim smile—"we'll be sure to hear about it when they do."

The next morning dawned, clear and brisk. Chef Maurice noted with satisfaction that Hamilton had finished off his midnight sow nut snack. There was no greater sin in his mind than an inadequate appetite.

Hamilton, who'd been running the perimeter, checking the fence in case the cows next door had invaded overnight, trotted over and nudged his empty bowl.

Chef Maurice shook his head. "They tell me I must feed you once a day only. Or else you become a fat *cochon*."

Hamilton poked his bowl again with his snout, and gave his new owner a look so pathetic that Walt Disney would have been proud.

"*Ai, d'accord*, but if you become fat, it is not my fault." Chef Maurice fished in his pockets, which were already bulging with sow nuts for this eventuality, and tossed a handful into Hamilton's bowl.

While the little pig wolfed down his morning treat, Chef Maurice bent over him to fit a new collar around Hamilton's stubby neck.

Gravel crunched and a large shadow loomed up behind them.

"And what do you think you are doing with that micro-pig?"

The voice was thoroughly thoroughbred, verging on braying, and belonged to a large tweed-upholstered woman with a clipboard.

This did not bode well, thought Chef Maurice. Nothing good in life, in his experience, ever came attached to a clipboard.

"We are going for a walk."

Her beady eyes lit up. "And do you have a Pig-walking Licence?"

"Ah, a joke, yes? *Très drôle, madame. Non*, I have not a pig-walking licence. Now, if I may—"

The clipboard was thrust at his chest.

"Section XVI, part iii, sub-paragraph d), of the Registration and Movement of Livestock code, as issued by the Department of Environment, Food and Rural Affairs. All pigs, whether owned as pets or forming part of a commercial herd, must apply for and obtain a CPN reference number. In addition, pigs owned for pets or as a hobby must carry a Pig-walking Licence from your local AHVA office, which must be—"

"And who are you, *madame?*"

At their feet, Hamilton gave the newcomer's boots a few exploratory snuffles.

"Helena Carter-Wright, founding member of the Friends of Our Fields Animal Welfare Trust. I was over at the sanctuary yesterday and Tara told me this little chap had found a home. So I thought I'd come see how he's settling in. You know a pig is for life, not—"

"*Oui, oui,* not just for dinner— I mean, Christmas." He glanced at the clipboard, then balanced it on top of Hamilton's kennel. "But I can write for my licence later, *non*? Hamilton and I, we have most important business to attend."

"I am afraid not," said Mrs Carter-Wright, in the voice of someone who is most delighted indeed. "No licence, no approved walks. Health and safety is paramount, Mr . . . "

"Manchot."

"Mr Manchot. Absolutely paramount. As a business owner yourself, working in the food industry, I'm sure you can appreciate that."

Chef Maurice scratched his head. He usually left all the health and risk assessment forms to Patrick, who dutifully filled them out and concluded each year that the biggest health and safety risk to Le Cochon Rouge was Chef Maurice himself. Last year, this had led to the triple-layered *tarte tatin* with a moat of flambéed Calvados brandy being removed from the menu—much to Dorothy's relief, as the char marks on the dining room ceiling had always been a chore to scrub off.

"Very well, *madame*. If you have a pencil . . . "

Mrs Carter-Wright smiled triumphantly. "That's the spirit. Here are all the forms you'll need. Just pop them in the post and in four to five weeks you'll—"

"*Weeks?*"

"Safety, Mr Manchot," said Mrs Carter-Wright, waving a severe finger. "Safety must always come first."

Chef Maurice appeared deflated. "*Très bien*. We must wait, Hamilton. Now I must start the morning preparations. *Bonne journée, madame*."

After the Land Rover had rolled out of the yard and away down the lane, Chef Maurice popped his head back around the corner and gestured at his pig.

"Psst, Hamilton, *viens ici*!" Hamilton stuck his nose out of his kennel, then trotted over.

Chef Maurice scooped him up and hurried into the dining room, where Dorothy was standing on a chair, dusting around the old stone fireplace. The building had once served as the old village pub, and the main dining room still retained all the original features.

"Dorothy, you have a little grand-niece, *n'est-ce pas?*"

"That's right, chef. Our Karen's eldest had her first back

in April, gorgeous little thing, quite knocks your socks off, she does. I can show you some photos if you'd—"

"Yes, yes, I remember, *un bébé très adorable*," said Chef Maurice hurriedly. "And they live in Beakley, I recall. Where is the exact address?"

"Oo, you know, I can never remember the number. It's just opposite the green, Mrs Cranshaw's old cottage, she's renting it out now on account of her bad—"

"*Merci!*"

The front door slammed, and pig and chef were gone.

Farnley Woods, twenty minutes west of Beakley, was a sprawling expanse of hilly woodland, sloping upwards from the winding main road. It was old forest land, populated by twisting oaks and towering sycamores, as well as beeches, birches, elms and the furry and fluttering creatures that called it home.

It was also the open-plan office for a small but growing number of professional foragers, who picked their way across the acres of woodland with empty backpacks, sturdy boots and a keen eye trained to the ground.

If there were truffles near Beakley, then Farnley Woods was where they'd be found.

Thus, a logical observer of recent events would not have been surprised to see Chef Maurice pull into the little dirt car park at the bottom of the woods.

They might, however, have spared a moment of surprise for the sight of his four-legged companion.

A few minutes later, Arthur's old but lovingly maintained Aston Martin pulled up alongside Chef Maurice's battered Citroën.

"Fine morning for a spot of truffle hunting," said Arthur, jumping out. He looked down at the little huddle sat beside Chef Maurice's steel-capped toes. "By golly, what have you done to Hamilton?"

Chef Maurice explained about Mrs Carter-Wright and her clipboard offensive.

"So you thought you'd disguise Hamilton as a six-month-old baby girl?"

Hamilton got to his trotters—daintily clad in two tiny pairs of wellington boots, one red, one sparkly pink—ran a little circle around them, then sat back down. He was wearing a bright pink fluffy hoodie.

"A dog," said Chef Maurice patiently. "Hamilton wears the disguise of a dog. The little ones that the Hollywood ladies carry in their handbags, *non*?"

In fact, he'd been quite disappointed when Geri, Dorothy's niece, had drawn the line at lending Hamilton a pair of pink diamante-encrusted sunglasses that, Chef Maurice had been convinced, would have been just the right accessory to complete '*le look*'.

"Whatever you say, old chap," said Arthur, as they started up the hill. "At least we can't lose him this way."

In the summer, Farnley Woods was full of weekend ramblers, young families, and couples looking for a little bit of seclusion, still convinced that there was something romantic, rather than prickly and slightly damp, about being around nature. Now, though, with autumn's gusty breezes and winter's dark nights just around the corner, the woods were empty of other walkers.

In front of them, Hamilton tugged at his lead, determined to show the world what a champion truffle hunter looked like.

"I never understood why you'd want to keep a dog in your handbag," mused Arthur. "Damned uncomfortable for the dog, I'd imagine, sitting on all those car keys, diaries, hairbrushes and whatnot. You should see the stuff Meryl keeps in hers. You could fit a good-sized Doberman in there, I reckon."

Hamilton gave a squeak and started digging at the roots of a nearby hazel.

"Good lad! Reckon he's found something already?"

Chef Maurice shook his head. "We are too close to the road. If the truffles are so easy to find, everyone would know, I think."

Sure enough, Hamilton's excavations produced half an old boot filled with mud. Chef Maurice patted him on the head and slipped him a sow nut.

They trudged on upwards. Recent showers had turned the ground into a treacherous mess of mud and soggy mulch. Chef Maurice could feel his knees creaking, and Arthur had fallen silent, apart from the occasional wheeze. Only Hamilton continued to forge ahead, now off his lead and running in dizzy circles ahead of them. He left no mound of leaves nor mouldering branch unturned, to the great consternation of the watching squirrel population.

Half an hour later, they were far off the well-trodden path and starting to wonder if they should have brought a map, a compass, and, most importantly in Chef Maurice's view, a bag of edible provisions, when they stumbled into a clearing. At the centre, surrounded by drifts of leaves, was a tall moss-covered rock that, if you half-closed your eyes and turned your head just so, looked just like a large standing bear.

"We call it The Bear," said a voice behind them. It belonged to a well-coiffed lady in her early fifties. She wore stout hiking boots and one of those padded green jackets with the leather elbow patches that managed to look both shapeless and very expensive at the same time. She was accompanied by a leggy grey poodle, wearing a matching green jacket, who attempted to look down its nose at them.

"That seems," said Chef Maurice, glancing at the rock, "a most appropriate name."

She looked like the type of woman who might take lunch with the likes of Mrs Carter-Wright. Just in case, he attempted to push Hamilton behind him with his foot.

"Goodness, aren't you Arthur Wordington-Smythe?" She turned her big blinking eyes on Arthur.

"At your service, madam," he said, lifting his hat.

"I simply adore your reviews. Such brilliant writing, I even tear out the ones I really like, you know, and stick them on the fridge. I get the England Observer every day, come rain or shine, but it's always your reviews I look forward to. I'm Brenda, by the way."

She held out a hand, but stopped halfway as her gaze fell to Chef Maurice's feet. "Oh my, is that a pig you have there?"

Chef Maurice considered denying it, but Brenda looked the type of well-bred outdoorsy Englishwoman who'd know her pigs from her pugs.

"He is a micro-pig, *madame*. His name is Hamilton." And because he couldn't stop himself, he added, "He is a champion truffle pig."

"How adorable!" said Brenda, bending down to pat Hamilton on the head. "More of a dog person myself, really, but isn't he precious?"

"Are you familiar with these woods, *madame*?"

"Like the back of my hands, I should say. I practically grew up in these woods. They back onto our land, you see," she said, waving vaguely into the distance.

Chef Maurice paused for a moment, weighing this woman up. "I do not suppose, *madame*, that you have seen such an item as this on your walks?" He unwrapped his handkerchief to reveal the remaining half truffle. The musty forest scent wafted around the clearing, and Hamilton started prancing up and down. The poodle looked up at the truffle and sneezed.

Brenda peered into the handkerchief. "Goodness, whatever is that? I thought it was a potato for a moment, but—"

"It is a truffle, *madame*."

"Oh, I've heard of those." She glanced at Arthur. "Restaurant critics are always talking about truffle this and truffle that. Never seen one up close, though." She gave it a sniff. "Can't say I see what the fuss is about, I'm afraid."

"You have not seen anything like this, then, here in these woods?"

"Not that I've ever noticed. And I think I'd have noticed something like that. Did you find it here?" She looked at him curiously.

"*Non*, but we have hope—" Chef Maurice stopped as Arthur jabbed him, hard, in the ribs. "*Non*, we did not. But we are most interested in these woods, even if there are *no truffles here*."

He shot Arthur a look that said: there, satisfied?

Brenda was staring up at the surrounding trees. "You know, my father collected all kinds of maps of these woods."

"Maps?" said Arthur quickly.

"Yes, all sorts. They go back decades, centuries even. If you're interested in Farnley Woods, you should come and take a look at them."

She reached into her handbag and pulled out a card.

Mrs Brenda Laithwaites. Laithwaites Manor, Farnley Woods, Oxfordshire.

"That is most kind of you, *madame*. We would be delighted to visit you." Chef Maurice dug around in his pockets for a moment, then looked beseechingly at Arthur. "*Mon ami*, do you, ah . . ."

Arthur sighed, opened his own wallet and extracted a card for Le Cochon Rouge.

"And do bring darling little—what was his name, oh yes—darling little Hamilton along with you too. Missy would love the company, I'm sure."

The grey poodle contrived to raise its nose even higher.

"Maurice, you really should buy a zipper for that big mouth of yours," said Arthur, as Brenda disappeared back into the woods, having extracted a promise that they would call on her soon. "And a cardholder, too, while you're at it."

"You think I should not have spoken of truffles? Ah, but now we have an invitation for tea!"

"Since when do you like tea?"

"I prefer an Englishman's tea to his coffee. But Madame Brenda also has maps of these woods. This could be very useful in our hunt."

"You think someone will have made a map marked 'Here Be Truffles'?"

"Ah, you joke, but a map of the trees, that is most useful. The white truffle of Alba"—he raised his lecturing finger—"is most fond of the hazelnut tree and the oak. We must look for these trees in particular, and there we will find truffles."

They walked on. The terrain here was rockier, the trees scrubbier, and huge drifts of leaves littered the ground and concealed a number of treacherous tree roots. Chef Maurice picked up a long stick and began poking around at the base of the nearby oak and hazel trees, as well as interrogating various suspicious mounds of moss.

"One never knows when you may find *une belle girolle*, or perhaps some oyster mushrooms," he explained.

Arthur peered under a large damp fallen trunk. "I find it's easier just to wait for the menu."

Hamilton continued to run in circles ahead of them, his little boots squelching through the mulch.

"Do you really think Hamilton is going to find these truffles of yours? Assuming they exist, of course."

"He has the soul of a truffle hunter, you will see," replied Chef Maurice staunchly.

"Soul maybe, but what about the nose?"

Hamilton gave a sudden squeak and started running towards the ridge above them. He weaved in and out of the moss-covered boulders, all of the same grey stone as The Bear earlier.

"You really . . . should have kept him . . . on a leash," breathed Arthur, as they hurried after the little pig.

"Bah. This is nothing. A little hill," said Chef Maurice, stomping onwards. "Meryl, she will thank me for taking you to exercise."

Up ahead, Hamilton had stopped at the edge of the ridge and was pacing back and forth, his curly tail quivering.

Chef Maurice was the first to reach him. "What is it, *mon petit* Hamilton?" He looked down into the gully. And swore.

"What is it? Is it truffles?" Arthur struggled up alongside him and looked down. "Bloody hell! Is that who I think it is?"

At the bottom of the gully, lying in a drift of leaves like a cast-aside rag doll, was the body of the late Ollie Meadows.

CHAPTER 7

PC Lucy stared down into the gully. She was not in the best of moods.

First off, and most definitely first, was the dead body. Not just any dead body, but the dead body of someone she knew. Well, not that she'd known Ollie on more than a passing basis, but still, she'd seen him around. And now here he was, face up in a ditch with a shotgun wound in the chest.

Second of all, there was Sergeant Burns, whose usual beat was Cowton town centre, but who'd somehow got it into his head that this was his investigation, despite Farnley being slap bang in PC Lucy's neck of the woods, as it were. He'd even gone as far as calling her 'lassie'. This was not helping her mood.

Lastly, there was Chef Maurice, who seemed to be developing a disconcerting habit of turning up in these situations.

Okay, so it was him and Arthur Wordington-Smythe who'd stumbled across the body—not literally, thank goodness—and phoned it in. But now the chef had snuck under the police cordon and was shuffling around behind the forensics team, such as it was, which consisted of a freckled young police officer called Alistair and a German shepherd called Fred. He was asking questions and, worst of all, making suggestions.

He was also carrying a small pig under one arm. The same pig that had tried to head-butt Fred on the nose when they'd first arrived at the scene.

"The body, it has been here many days?" said Chef Maurice, watching PC Alistair take pictures and carefully scrape bits of forest floor into plastic tubs.

"At least a couple of days, we think. It's Wednesday today, so that means—"

"Alistair! Please refrain from discussing details with members of the public."

"Sorry, miss." He saw the look on her face. "Uh, I mean, PC Gavistone."

Chef Maurice wandered round to the other side to get a better view of PC Alistair's work.

"And it is certain that Monsieur Ollie was murdered?"

"I think you'll find, Mr Manchot," said PC Lucy drily, "that people don't tend to go around shooting themselves with shotguns. At least not in the chest."

Dammit. She hadn't meant to engage. "Ahem. That is, the police will certainly be carrying out a thorough investigation. We appreciate your concern, and thank you for your co-operation earlier with your witness statements. We'll be in touch if we have further questions."

At least the statements had been easy enough. Having most definitely absolutely without-a-doubt secured a pig-walking licence this morning—whatever that was—Chef Maurice and Arthur had taken a leisurely stroll up into Farnley Woods. They'd met a nice lady walking her dog who, in their measured opinion, did not appear to be a shotgun-wielding maniac. Then they had found Ollie in the gully. Or at least, the pig had found the gully, and then they'd found Ollie.

Had they known the victim? Arthur knew him by sight, but viewed Ollie as the type who kept himself to himself. Plus, the forager had only lived in the village for a few years, which was no time at all by Beakley standards.

As for Chef Maurice, Ollie was his wild herb and mushroom supplier, which seemed all above board. No, there hadn't been any bad feeling between the two, and anyway Chef Maurice pointed out most emphatically that a chef could not go around shooting his suppliers, even when they annoyed him; you'd soon run out of suppliers. Yes, Ollie had failed to make his most recent delivery, but this was now completely understandable in the light of today's findings.

"So you and Mr Wordington-Smythe are now free to go." She put emphasis on those last two words, but they fell on uninterested ears.

Chef Maurice squatted down next to Alistair.

"Was there anything of interest in his pockets?"

"Not that we've found, sir. He had a phone, of course—"

"Alistair!"

"Sorry, miss."

"And these marks here on Monsieur Ollie's jacket—"

PC Lucy had had enough. "Mr Manchot! The police are more than capable of handling this investigation. If you'll *please* step outside the cordoned area, we cannot have members of the public contaminating the crime scene. Especially not those carrying livestock!"

Chef Maurice retreated under the cordon. Hamilton, from under his arm, gave her a reproachful grunt.

PC Lucy folded her arms and watched PC Alistair prepare a stretcher for the body.

This was going to be her first real homicide investigation. They didn't get many of those in these parts. Her superiors would be watching her closely.

She really hoped she wasn't going to make a pig's ear of it.

Arthur sat on a rock outside the cordoned area, facing away from the gully and looking as green as the moss he was sat on.

Chef Maurice bounded up, Hamilton trotting at his feet. "*Mon ami*, you must come see, it is most interesting what they do!"

"I assure you, I'm perfectly happy where I am, thank you very much," said Arthur, staring fixedly at the tree straight in front of him.

"They say he has been there for a number of days."

"Lovely."

"Which seems correct. Both Madame Eldridge and Mademoiselle Lucy spoke to him on Saturday morning, after the first break-in. Then he was not seen again. It is therefore likely that he was shot on Saturday."

"Fancy that."

"The state of Monsieur Ollie's jacket, I found it most odd."

"Covered in blood, you mean?" Arthur turned a little more grey. "No, forget I said that."

"*Non, non*, we are not interested in blood."

"We aren't? Thank goodness for that," said Arthur weakly.

"*Non*, you see, the long scratches on the jacket, all on the back, none on the front, it is suggesting to me that Monsieur Ollie was dragged a certain distance to this place."

"So?"

"Why did they not simply bury him?"

Arthur pushed his heel into the ground. The soil was rock hard, once you got through the thin layer of mud. "Perhaps they forgot their shovel."

Chef Maurice appeared to look at his friend for the first time. "You do not look well, *mon ami*. Come, we must find you a drink."

Arthur allowed himself to be heaved to his feet. "I think I saw a pub back down in Farnley," he volunteered.

"Pah! Why drink beer when we have the finest aged cognac?"

They trudged on, skidding occasionally as they descended.

"You've got cognac in your car?"

"But of course!"

"Maurice, do drink-driving laws mean nothing to you?"

"I am shocked. I have never thought to drink and drive!"

"Oh, really?"

"One must always pull over. And it is just a little sip, just to warm the body on a cold day . . . "

Arthur let this one go. Given Chef Maurice's somewhat ballistic driving skills, a nip of brandy was the least of his concerns.

"I'll get my car tomorrow morning," he said, as he climbed into Chef Maurice's passenger seat after having applied a generous dose of cognac to his frazzled nerves. Behind him, Hamilton shot him a baleful glare, having been relegated to his basket in the back. "Onwards to Beakley?"

"*Un moment.*"

Chef Maurice leaned over, flipped open the glove compartment and extracted a box of crackers, a small wheel of something that looked like Camembert but smelt like a bag of rugby players' socks, a wooden-handled knife and a large red-and-white-checked handkerchief.

"One does not know when one may miss a meal," said Chef Maurice, spreading a lump of cheese across a cracker. He waved the knife at Arthur. "You are hungry?"

"Not in the slightest," squeaked Arthur. He wound down the window and stuck his head out. "Though I think I could manage a little more cognac . . . "

One box of crackers and three-quarters of the cheese later, Chef Maurice swung out of the car park and pointed the car in the opposite direction to Beakley.

"Where are we going now?" It was only mid-morning still, but Arthur felt like days had passed since he'd last been in bed. A nap at this point would not go amiss.

"To the Helpful Paws animal house."

"See, I told you getting a micro-pig was a damn silly idea." There was a high-pitched squeal from behind. "They don't do returns, you know."

Chef Maurice gave him a puzzled look. "Returns? I have no wish to return Hamilton. I go to enquire about a dog."

Arthur leant back in his seat and closed his eyes. "Go on. Tell me why a dog."

"It is not obvious?"

"No, it is not obvious."

"Think about it, *mon ami*. We know that Monsieur Ollie found truffles. Now we ask: did he get down on his knees and dig for them? *Non!* He must have a dog. Or a pig. But I think most likely a dog, as we would hear if he had a pig. Do you see now?"

When Arthur remained silent, Chef Maurice continued, "We found Monsieur Ollie, but we have not found his dog. Therefore, we go to find his dog. Think, *mon ami*. A trained truffle dog! Think what treasures we will find with this dog!"

There was another indignant squeal from the back of the car.

"And we can use *le chien* to train Hamilton, of course."

"Hmm," said Arthur. "If you're right, the police are bound to be looking for Ollie's dog too. Evidence and whatnot. Might have got a good bite out of the murderer, you never know."

"Ah." Chef Maurice looked momentarily deflated. "Perhaps they will then allow me to borrow the dog?"

"I don't think you're on their list of favourites at the moment, especially not with PC Gavistone."

"I made some most helpful suggestions."

"No doubt."

They left Hamilton in the car with the windows cracked open and a handful of sow nuts to keep him busy. He turned up his nose and gave a meaningful stare towards the glove compartment.

The spotty-faced youth from yesterday was mending a fence in the outdoor kennel yard.

"Can I help?" he said, eyes fixed on the task.

"We are looking for a truffle dog," said Chef Maurice importantly.

The youth looked up. "Look, I already told you, dogs and chocolate don't—"

Arthur decided it was time to employ some tact— otherwise known as stopping Chef Maurice from talking.

"What my friend means," he said hurriedly, "is that we're looking for a dog called Truffles. He belongs to a friend. He went missing"—it was Wednesday today, and Ollie had last been seen on Saturday—"at least seventy-two hours ago."

The youth frowned. "That's two days ago, right?"

"Um, possibly more like three . . . "

"Right. What kind of dog is it?"

"Um." Arthur hadn't thought this far. He shot a look at Chef Maurice, who shrugged. He recalled seeing Ollie out and about in the village with a dog. And there'd been a dog basket in the cottage. But it had clearly been a particularly nondescript dog.

"Not a big dog," he hazarded. "But not too small either. Medium, perhaps."

"Right. And colour?"

"Um. Brown?"

"O-*kay*, a medium maybe-brown dog," said the youth, giving him an odd look. "In the last three days. I'll go see what I can do."

"It might be black, actually," called Arthur, as the door swung closed.

In the kennel opposite them, an old basset hound gave them an unimpressed look.

Eventually, Tara appeared through the doors, a broad smile on her face as she bore down on them.

"How lovely to see you both again! How's Hamilton settling into his new home?"

"Very well, *madame*," said Chef Maurice. "But it is not about Hamilton we come to speak to you today. Your *collègue* has mentioned our friend's missing dog?"

"Yes, but I'm afraid your friend has stolen a march on you. I'm surprised he didn't already tell you, really. He

64

turned up on Sunday, poor little thing—the dog, I mean. He'd been lost in the woods, absolutely covered in mud, and a nice couple found him and brought him in. We'd just got him cleaned up when your friend turned up."

"This was Sunday too?" Chef Maurice looked in confusion at Arthur.

"Yes, I remember because we didn't even have time to set up a file for him. We took a picture, though." She held up a Polaroid of a medium-sized scruffy brown dog of indeterminate breed. "Is this him?"

Arthur nodded. That was definitely Ollie's dog. He remembered the mutt now, a well-behaved little fellow by all accounts. But Ollie hadn't been seen since Saturday morning. And here he was, apparently picking up his lost dog on Sunday at the Pet Sanctuary. What had he been doing in the time in between? And more importantly, what had happened after?

"And the dog's owner— I mean, our friend," said Arthur. "Just to check, was he a tall, young fellow, with a bit of stubble, likes wearing hiking-type gear, generally looks a bit worse for wear?"

Tara tilted her head. "Sorry, I don't quite follow . . . "

"The man who came on Sunday?" said Chef Maurice. "For the dog?"

"Yes, I know, but he was nothing like your friend you just described. Tall, yes, but definitely not young. In his fifties, I'd say, big dark beard, had a bit of an accent though I couldn't quite place it . . . "

Arthur and Chef Maurice looked at each other in horror. Someone had beaten them to it.

"That man, *madame*, was not the owner of the dog."

"Oh, he definitely was," said Tara confidently. "He had all the paperwork, the dog passport, pictures of the two of them together. We take a lot of care about this kind of thing—" She noticed them staring at her. "Is something wrong?"

CHAPTER 8

They motored back to Beakley in a confused silence. Hamilton, apparently satisfied that they had not adopted a dog, or worse, a second pig, dozed happily in the back.

"This is very bad, *mon ami*."

"It is? I still haven't the foggiest what's going on."

"We are not the only ones to know about Monsieur Ollie and the truffles. Why else would someone steal his truffle dog?"

"Well, I wouldn't call it—"

"Snatched from below our noses!"

"It was three days ago, Maurice. Our noses weren't even out of bed. What I can't figure out is how the chap put together all the paperwork."

"There are ways," said Chef Maurice darkly. "But that is not the worst. Think, how would this man know to look for Monsieur Ollie's dog?"

Arthur drummed his fingers on the dashboard. "Well, maybe—"

"*Non*, not maybe. It is *évident, mon ami*. Who would know that Monsieur Ollie's dog was lost in the woods? The man who shot Monsieur Ollie in the first place!"

Arthur turned to look at him. "You honestly think someone would bump off Ollie just to steal his dog?"

"And his patch of truffles, remember. A most valuable combination."

"Seems a bit far-fetched to me. This is the Cotswolds, not Sicily, Maurice."

"Ah, but the man, he had an accent, *non*? That is suspicious."

"Pot, kettle . . . " muttered Arthur.

There were a couple of police cars parked outside Ollie's cottage and a police cordon across the front door. A small crowd had gathered on the sidelines, just in case it turned out there was something worth seeing. Chef Maurice spotted Mrs Eldridge up at the front, arms crossed and foot tapping, peeved to have been denied inside access this time around.

He dropped Arthur off at the Wordington-Smythe cottage and headed back to Le Cochon Rouge. Hamilton jumped out of the car and ran back to his pen, presumably to catch the cows up on today's adventures. In the kitchens, lunch service had been successfully concluded and dinner prep was quietly getting underway.

Chef Maurice rummaged around in the walk-in fridge and returned with a bag of apples, a large *tarte normande* and a small jug of cream.

He tossed the bag of apples at Alf. "Peeled, cored, thinly sliced. Patrick, a *pâte sucrée* for the base is needed. We will need a new *tarte normande* this evening."

"I thought we already had—" started Patrick, then noticed the apple tart in Chef Maurice's hand. "*Oui*, chef. One *tarte normande*."

Chef Maurice doused his impromptu late lunch with cream, then wandered over to the hobs. He stuck his nose over a pot of reducing stock, sniffed, then turned down the flame one notch.

The kitchen door burst open.

"You'll never guess what!"

It was Dorothy, cheeks flushed from the heat of gossip hot off the press.

"Annie just dropped round with the linen, and she just heard it from Charlie, who heard from his brother over in Cowton. There's been a murder up in Farnley Woods. A murder!"

"Cor!" said Alf.

"That's awful," said Patrick.

Chef Maurice opened his mouth, then closed it. Dorothy would never forgive him if he stole her thunder now.

"And you'll never guess who it was. Ollie Meadows! I said to Annie, if anyone was going to be murdered around here, it'd be that scallywag Ollie, always sneaking around in people's gardens. Not to speak ill of the dead, of course," she added primly.

"Blimey!" said Alf, absentmindedly biting into an apple. He'd moved to Beakley from the hamlet of Little Goving, population six. Life in the big village was currently exceeding all his expectations. "How'd it happen? Who did it?"

"Well, of course they don't know yet," said Dorothy, in the tone of someone who has watched their fair share of murder mysteries and knows how these things go. "But they know he was shot, right in the chest, they say. Puts a chill up you, that does. We all thought he'd just run off with some girl, and then bam, he turns up dead as a doorknob. Makes you think of locking your doors and getting a big Rottweiler, it does. And think about the poor soul that found him . . . "

"*Oui*, it was most horrific," said Chef Maurice, tipping the last of the cream over his plate. "Arthur, he was almost sick. I think he does not possess the constitution for *le crime*."

He looked up at his staff's open mouths. "You do not know? It was we who found *le pauvre* Ollie, on our walk with Hamilton this morning."

Dorothy's face was a battlefield of emotion. On one hand, her boss had completely upstaged her, but on the other hand, she now had access to a genuine crime scene witness, which was one up on Annie, who'd only heard about it because her boyfriend's brother was a police constable over in Cowton, and he hadn't even been there.

In the end, the lure of premium-quality gossip won out.

"Oh my, that must have been terrible," she cried. "Sit

70

down, chef, let me make you a cup of coffee, and you can tell us all about it. It's a terrible burden to carry, I tell you, to keep it all in. Best get it out, I always say."

So the morning's sorry tale was rehashed, with extra dash and daring on Chef Maurice's part, and some light embellishment of his conversation with PC Lucy.

"Lucy?" said Patrick, looking up from prepping a tray of pork belly. "The policewoman who lives down near the green? Blonde? Er . . . " He waved his hands. "Nice and . . . uh . . . " His ears were going red.

"That's her," said Dorothy, with a grin. "Comes here every week for the Sunday roast. Always has the lamb."

"She comes for dinner too, sometimes," added Chef Maurice, who liked to get out into the dining room during service to shake hands with regulars, top up wine glasses and inject a little Gallic bonhomie into the room. And to make sure they all cleaned their plates, of course.

"Does she, um, come along with anyone?" said Patrick with extreme nonchalance, eyes focussed on scoring the pork belly all over.

"She's often with a girlfriend, another police lady, I think," said Dorothy, winking at Chef Maurice. "Not half as pretty, in my mind."

"Right." Patrick bent over, salting the pork with a look of ferocious concentration.

"So *do* the police know who did it?" said Dorothy, turning back to Witness Number One.

Chef Maurice shook his head.

"Of course, they'll have to read his will," said Dorothy, sudden criminal expert. "Find out who benefits the most, and that's your murderer, nine times out of ten, I tell you."

"Cor, that's clever," said Alf. Beakley was turning out to be an education and a half.

"Monsieur Ollie did not seem the type to have a will."

"Do you have a will, chef?"

"Of course." His was fairly simple. To Arthur, he'd leave his Citroën and cookbooks. Patrick would get Le Cochon Rouge, should he still be sous-chef.

He wondered who should get Hamilton now.

"I heard someone broke into his cottage, twice," said Dorothy. "Might have been looking for that will. There's always a surprise will. Leaving everything to the maid, or the like. Or sometimes it could be a forgery . . . "

Chef Maurice thought about Ollie's stolen map. Surely Ollie wouldn't have written his will on a map?

"Can't imagine he had much to leave, though, always griping on about his bills and all. His cottage was a right mess, Annie said. Just a load of old plants and those mushrooms of his."

Chef Maurice dropped his spoon and glanced up at the clock. It might not be too late . . .

"Patrick!"

"*Oui*, chef?" Patrick shut the walk-in fridge, having bedded down the salt-and-sage-rubbed pork belly for a good flavourful rest.

"Come." He put a friendly arm around his sous-chef's

shoulder. "I have a special task for you that I think you will most enjoy . . . "

Get hold of the truffles. Don't mention the truffles.

Patrick tried to hold these two thoughts in his head as he hurried down through Beakley towards Ollie Meadows' cottage.

It wasn't stealing, Chef Maurice had said. They were doing the world of gastronomy a favour, even. What would a police station do with a sack of white truffles? Have them with weak tea and digestive biscuits?

Patrick's thoughts took a detour through a land of savoury beignets drizzled in truffle-infused oil.

He wouldn't have to lie, either, chef had said. Similar to using truffle shavings, it just paid to be economical with the truth. If someone came out and said "Is this bag of truffles we found in the fridge worth thousands of pounds?" he'd have to answer honestly. But it wasn't his fault that a bag of white truffles looked a good deal like a bag of small, dusty potatoes.

His thoughts also drifted to a certain blonde police-woman. He'd seen her around and about the village, but working six-day weeks and spending all his free time developing new recipes, which he tried to slip onto the menu without Chef Maurice complaining too much, left him little chance to get to know his Beakley neighbours.

He took another mental detour to visit the fried-squid-and-piquillo-pepper starter he'd been working on lately.

All in all, Patrick's head was so full of thoughts that his feet brought him all the way to Ollie's back gate before he realised he hadn't worked out what he was, in fact, going to say.

A freckle-faced young policeman looked up from examining the broken door lock.

"Can I help, sir?"

"I was wondering if I could have a word with, um, Miss"—he realised he had no idea what her surname was—"um, Lucy?"

"That's PC Gavistone to you," said a voice from inside the cottage, and PC Lucy appeared at the door. Her hair was straying from its bun, framing her face in a halo of wisps, and the state of her uniform suggested she'd spent the last few hours down on her knees in dusty cupboards.

"Well?" she demanded.

Patrick felt his throat dry up. A degree in molecular biology, a short-lived career in software development, then successive jobs in professional kitchens mostly staffed by large, sweaty men, had left Patrick in his early thirties with a resume containing a distinct lack of detail in the Talking To Women section.

Especially not attractive young women who carried their own truncheons.

"I'm, uh, I've come from Le Cochon Rouge, I'm the sous-chef there and—"

"Perfect!" PC Lucy smiled—but tigers smiled too, didn't they? thought Patrick—and held up a hand. "Just wait there a moment."

She disappeared into the cottage and came back with a small woven sack. The smell of truffles drifted out into the back garden, an unspoken accusation.

"I don't suppose you know what these are?" she said sweetly, holding open the bag. "Being a chef and all?"

Get hold of the truffles. Don't mention the truffles.

"Um, they could be Maris Pipers, they're good for making mash and roast potat—"

"And *I* might be the Queen of Sheba."

The smile vanished. PC Lucy held out a scrap of paper, covered in familiar loopy handwriting. Patrick had a sinking feeling.

"I found this in the sack. You know anything about this?"

Patrick took the note.

Cher monsieur Meadows,

I owe you payment for: 1 bag wild mushrooms, small. 1 bunch bananas, squashed (these I sat on when your table overturned on me). 1 truffle, large, white.

Please return from being missing soon, or I will require a new mushroom supplier.

M. Maurice Manchot

PS: Your kitchen floor requires a sweep. It is most unpleasant to sit upon.

Patrick tugged at the collar of his chef's jacket, which had suddenly become dangerously tight.

"Well, we did make a banana soufflé yesterday, which seemed a bit odd for this time of year . . . "

He trailed off as PC Lucy's blue eyes bored into him.

"Tell Mr Manchot I'll be along to speak to him later," she said, eyes narrowed. "And tell him I'd appreciate it if he could refrain from eating all the evidence he removed from a murder investigation, too."

Patrick thought about yesterday's omelette breakfast.

"I'll do my best. I guess I'll be, um, going now . . . ?"

PC Lucy nodded curtly and swung around without a backwards glance.

At least, thought Patrick, he hadn't mentioned the truffles. Which meant he'd achieved at least one of his two aims.

And she said she'd be along to the restaurant later. Giving him a second chance to attempt to interact.

He hoped he wouldn't mess it up again. Given their meeting just now, he rather doubted he'd get a chance at a close encounter of the third kind.

The problem with Chef Maurice, thought PC Lucy later that evening, was the way that any situation he was involved in managed to slip through your fingers faster than a well-oiled ferret.

She'd stormed up to the back door of Le Cochon Rouge, bag of truffles in one hand, ready with a stern lecture about withholding information from the police and perverting the course of justice.

She'd expected him to posture, to wave his hands and argue his case. But the chef had seemed almost contrite, as much as one could tell under that giant moustache. He apologised profusely, the way only a Frenchman can, and invited her in for dinner.

They sat at the kitchen table and, somehow, over a glass of good white wine and truffle-covered linguine, she found herself handing over another large truffle from the sack— after all, what were they going to do with them down at the station?—in exchange for everything he had found out about Ollie's missing dog and its mysterious rescuer.

"Tall, dark beard, in his fifties, possibly foreign," she repeated, noting this down. Her head felt a little dizzy, and she wondered if she should have accepted the second glass of white Burgundy. Still—she glanced at her watch—she was technically off-duty.

"And they didn't even get his name?"

"Mademoiselle Tara said it was something Spanish or Italian. Ending with an *oh*."

Well, that narrowed it down. Tomorrow she'd have to go over there and check out the CCTV, if they even had it. She didn't have high hopes on that count, though—animal rescue homes were not exactly a hotbed of crime, apart from the crime of abandonment, of course.

"More pasta?" said Chef Maurice, waving a fork at the pan. He was already on his fourth helping.

PC Lucy looked down at her large but empty plate and willpower failed her. Anyway, she told herself, she hadn't eaten much all day, what with the new case and all.

"Was anything more of interest found at Monsieur Ollie's home?"

"Not much," she found herself saying, "apart from finding a few more stashes of cash around the house. He'd clearly been doing very well for himself lately." She picked up a piece of truffle with her fork and stared at it. "Now I can see why. How much was he charging for these?"

Chef Maurice's face darkened. "He had not offered me a single truffle! *Quelle effronterie!* I, who have bought from him since the first day of his *entreprise*. When I find out which chefs he has been selling to—"

"He did say he had something new for us, chef."

Lucy looked up. It was the sous-chef from earlier. She hadn't caught his name, but now she had time to notice him properly, it struck her that he rather resembled a curly-haired Clark Kent. Perhaps a little less square-jawed, but as he scrubbed out a large stockpot over the sinks, with his chef's jacket rolled up past his elbows, she couldn't help but notice the muscles on his forearms gleaming in the soap suds . . .

She blinked. It must be the wine, she decided.

Chef Maurice was still on his tirade. "We should have been the first! It is an insult, an impertinence, a—"

"Can we even afford to have a truffle dish, chef?"

Chef Maurice glared at him. "That is not the point!"

Bzzzzz! PC Lucy pulled out her phone.

"PC Gavistone?" It was Alistair. "We've located the victim's vehicle. It's in the woods right behind Farnley village."

"Understood. I'll be right there."

She stood up, and the kitchen swayed. Yep, that second glass had definitely been a mistake.

Chef Maurice jumped to his feet. "You must not drive, *mademoiselle*. Let me get my keys—"

A hand clamped down on his shoulder. "With respect, chef, not on your life. I'll drive, uh, PC Gavistone where she needs to go."

"It's okay, you can call me Lucy." Why was she grinning like an idiot? "Sorry, I didn't quite catch—"

"Patrick."

Patrick. Not Pat. She didn't know why, but she rather liked that.

"Well, thank you, Patrick. I don't know what got into me tonight. I don't usually drink during the week."

"Chef generally has that effect on people." A wry smile passed over his face.

They found Chef Maurice standing by the front door, holding a tin of biscuits.

"You must eat more, *mademoiselle*," he said sternly, staring her up and down. "It is not good for a young woman to, how do you say, have a look of hunger."

She looked down at her waistline, surprised. She'd never considered herself at risk of sporting a waif-like look. Sure, the job kept her trim enough, though any beneficial result was possibly less due to exercise and more due to the Cowton and Beakley Constabulary's minuscule budget, which stretched to cheap tea and one small box of assorted biscuits per week. And the Chief Inspector always nicked the chocolate ones before anyone else could get there.

He handed her the tin, then followed them outside, pulling on his hat and coat.

"Mr Manchot, this is an official police investigation," she said, with as much gravity as she could muster on a full stomach of pasta and white Burgundy.

"This is my car, and that is my sous-chef," said Chef Maurice, climbing into the front passenger seat. "Do we go or not?"

She sighed and climbed into the back.

"It'll be okay," said Patrick, revving up the engine of the little Citroën. "Chef can be quite unobtrusive when he wants to be."

"And how often is that?"

"I'll let you know if it ever happens."

CHAPTER 9

PC Alistair stood in the road at the bottom of Farnley Woods, shielding his eyes from the approaching headlights. He motioned them down a short dirt track to a scrubby field, hidden by dense vegetation from the main road and the small huddle of cottages that made up the hamlet of Farnley.

PC Lucy jumped out and strode over to the abandoned car, which was currently overrun with police constables wielding torches.

Chef Maurice and Patrick stood off to one side, far enough from the reach of PC Lucy's sharp tongue, but near enough to hear everything going on.

It appeared that Ollie's car was disappointingly bare of clues to its owner's sudden demise. There were a few empty plastic crates in the back, presumably waiting for the day's mushroom find, a pile of old newspapers, and yet another pair of muddy boots. There was also a half-empty box of dog treats in the glove compartment.

Chef Maurice brushed a few biscuit crumbs off his coat. "*Très intéressant*," he said, glancing around the overgrown field.

"Yes, chef?" Patrick tried not to stare as PC Lucy bent all the way over to inspect the back seat of Ollie's car.

"There is a free car parking on the main road, just twenty metres from this place, but Monsieur Ollie chooses to put his car here. I ask why?"

"Guess he didn't want people to know he was foraging here?"

"But Farnley Woods is a permitted ground. A bag of mushrooms, a basket of herbs, what is there to hide?"

"Poaching, then?"

"Bah, there is no money in the poaching of game. The businessmen from London, they come here to shoot many birds, but they do not want to get their hands dirty after. How do you think we have such good prices for pheasant?"

PC Lucy had now finished with the car and was conversing in low tones with PC Alistair.

"Come, I cannot hear."

They inched closer, staring nonchalantly at the moonlit trees around them.

"Been round to three of the Farnley cottages already, miss, just before you arrived. None of them claim to know anything about the victim's car."

"Did they happen to know Ollie?"

"Only by sight, they said. And I got the feeling they didn't like him coming round here."

"How come? Because of the foraging?"

"Suppose so, miss. Some people think just because they

live near some woods, they're the only ones allowed in them."

PC Lucy hiccupped discreetly. "Do you think any of them might be responsible for those notes he received?"

"Doubt it, miss. They're all pretty old folk, quiet like, most of them were in bed when I knocked."

She sighed. "Well, let's not keep the last ones waiting, then."

The sole inhabitant of Grove Cottage was at least fifty years younger than her neighbours. She had the pale look of a natural redhead, and her carefully manicured fingers played nervously with the silver leaf pendant around her neck.

No, she didn't know anything about the car in the field. No one went up that way; she didn't even know who owned that land.

"What about Mr Meadows? Did you know him at all?"

Mrs Kristine Hart's eyes flickered, then she shook her head. "Not very well. He used to come round knocking sometimes, selling mushrooms and herbs when he collected more than he expected."

"And when was the last time you saw him?"

Another flicker. "I don't know, at least a couple of weeks ago, I think."

PC Lucy looked down at her notebook. "What about your husband, Mrs Hart? Did he know Mr Meadows?"

"I don't think so. Nick's away on business most of the week."

"Can we speak to him now?"

A faint smile. "I'm afraid he's in Cologne at the moment. He flew out last Friday."

Chef Maurice nudged Patrick. "Most convenient," he muttered. "Monsieur Ollie, he was last seen on the Saturday."

Patrick gave him a puzzled look. "So, just because her husband wasn't here on Saturday, he must be involved in the murder?"

"*Exactement!*"

They were standing up against the window to the front lounge. Through the open curtains, they could admire Mrs Hart's tasteful, stylish furnishings. A bold canvas of modern art hung over the fireplace, and the shelves were sparsely decorated with abstract sculptures. The only jarring note was a vase of drooping wild flowers on the mantelpiece. Chef Maurice would have expected a single orchid, or an unusual cactus, perhaps.

"Well, thank you for your time, Mrs Hart," said PC Lucy, pulling out a card. "If you think of anything else, please do give us a call."

After the door clicked shut, PC Lucy spun around to face them. Patrick took a quick step backwards.

"Mr Manchot! I'd appreciate it if you didn't stand there making completely baseless accusations at members of the public."

"Ah. But if my accusations had a base—"

"Not then, either."

They walked back to the car, PC Lucy two strides ahead.

"She lies," murmured Chef Maurice.

"She wouldn't do that," said Patrick, aghast.

"Eh? *Non*, not Mademoiselle Lucy. The other. *La belle* Madame Hart."

"I didn't think she was that good-looking," said Patrick, rather louder than necessary.

Back in the field, PC Lucy pulled out two more cards. "I need to head to the station now. I'll get a lift with Alistair. Here's my number, call me if you think of anything else. *Call*, Mr Manchot. Do not *do*. Please."

Chef Maurice nodded affably. He was enjoying himself immensely. He had truffles to find, a new four-legged friend to train, and now a murder case to solve. Cooking was all very well, but he felt he could do with a little more mental stimulation at this point in life.

Besides, he thought, watching Patrick carefully place PC Lucy's card in his wallet, he had his sous-chef's love life to watch out for. If he could solve this case, it would surely raise his whole kitchen crew in PC Lucy's esteem.

Autumn at Le Cochon Rouge was definitely looking up.

Early next morning, the truffle hunt resumed.

Chef Maurice left Patrick and Alf plucking the morning pheasant delivery out in the yard, surrounded by a slew of flying feathers, and loaded Hamilton into the back seat of his car. The little pig was once again kitted out in his anti-pig-walking-licence disguise.

They stopped in the village to pick up Arthur and Horace, who had been persuaded to forgo his post-breakfast snooze in order to protect his master from any murderous shotguns. Plus he'd heard there would be opportunity to chase, or at least lumber after, a few squirrels.

"Funny business, all this," said Arthur, after Chef Maurice caught him up on the last night's activities. "Abandoned cars, shootings, dead bodies in the woods. Not really what people come to the Cotswolds for. Visitor numbers will slump, mark my words."

Chef Maurice waved a hand at the road. "Then why are there so many people here?"

The little clearing at the bottom of Farnley Woods was packed with cars, mostly of the type that rattled at over forty miles an hour and required a good thump to the bonnet to get started on a cold winter's day.

The local pensioners were out in force.

It seemed there was nothing like a bit of murder to get the nearby villages' older population out into the fresh air. Some of the more enterprising senior sleuths had even brought along magnifying glasses, while the others were relying on their spare pairs of varifocals. Walking sticks and plastic sandwich bags at the ready, the pensioners were busy in the woods, unearthing a variety of squashed cans and long-lost woollen gloves, and the odd piece of loose change. One old lady was diligently scraping some suspicious-looking red paint into a paper bag.

"Might be blood," whispered her companion, looking around to check no one else had noticed their discovery.

Thankfully, the steep slopes, uneven ground, and lack

of tea rooms and toilet facilities meant that the crowd hadn't wandered too much further than shouting distance from the main road. Chef Maurice and Arthur struck out towards the depths of Farnley Woods, with Hamilton running ahead and Horace bringing up the rear guard.

A truffle-less forty minutes later, either by accident or unconscious design, they found themselves back at The Bear.

"Some people say the smell of truffles resembles the scent of male pigs, if you follow my meaning," said Arthur, watching Hamilton sniff around the mossy rocks. "Maybe you should have got a female pig instead. Ouch," he added, as Hamilton head-butted him on the ankle.

"It will take time," said Chef Maurice, regarding his new colleague indulgently. "But he will prove himself. It is certain."

There was a flash of neon yellow from between the trees on the far side of the clearing.

"*Bonjour!*" shouted Chef Maurice, cupping his hands around his mouth. "Is somebody there?"

Arthur, on the other hand, had ducked behind The Bear.

In the distance, there was the faint sound of snapping twigs, then silence.

"'Allo?" No answer. Chef Maurice picked up a large branch. "Stay here, *mon ami*, and guard Hamilton. Come, Horace."

Horace looked up at him and decided he didn't get enough dog biscuits for this. He lay down in the leaves and yawned theatrically.

Branch raised, Chef Maurice stepped quietly into the thick woods.

A strip of bright yellow peeked through some bushes up ahead.

"I can see you," he shouted. "Come out!"

"Dammit," a female voice whispered. "Alistair, I told you not to wear that thing up here."

PC Lucy stepped out from behind a nearby tree, a smile of pleasant surprise plastered across her face.

"Mr Manchot, what a . . . pleasant surprise. Are you walking Hamilton again?"

PC Alistair crawled his way out of a bush. He was wearing a large high-visibility jacket and a sheepish look.

Chef Maurice looked past their shoulders with interest. A small flat area of trees had been cordoned off. Squirrels darted back and forth, acorns in paws, stopping here and there to dig frenetically. Horace would have had a field day.

"Ah, so you have discovered the location of Monsieur Ollie's shooting?"

PC Lucy narrowed her eyes. "Please tell me that's just a guess."

Chef Maurice pointed at the clear plastic bag in PC Alistair's hands, which contained a blood-and-mud-splattered grey cap, the type Ollie always used to wear. Too late, the young man tried to hide it behind his back.

"Honestly, Alistair!"

"Sorry, miss."

"Good morning, officers," said Arthur, struggling through the undergrowth, dragging Horace on his lead. "I thought I heard your voices. Sorry for the delay. I was just, um, tying a shoelace. Found anything interesting?"

"We have found the location where Monsieur Ollie was shot," said Chef Maurice, beaming. PC Lucy rolled her eyes.

"Ah, capital work. So you were right, old chap. He *was* dragged into that gully. But the question is why?"

PC Alistair opened his mouth, then clamped it shut again, with a sideways look at PC Lucy.

"You can tell them," she said wearily. "It's all speculation at this point anyway."

"We reckon we're too near the road here, sir."

"Road?"

"The A323 runs just along up there." Alistair pointed behind him. "You can't see it but you can hear the lorries go by if you listen. We reckon whoever shot Ollie was worried someone might have heard and come to investigate. And Crinklewood Lodge is only half a mile over that way, and Laithwaites Manor backs onto the woods not far up there."

Chef Maurice perked up at the mention of Laithwaites Manor. "Have you spoken to those who live there yet? If not, I could perhaps—"

"Enquiries are proceeding, Mr Manchot."

"Please, you must call me Maurice."

"As you wish. Now if you gentlemen will excuse us . . ."

PC Lucy and Alistair continued combing the ground. Chef Maurice and Arthur stood and watched for a while, but no further discoveries seemed forthcoming.

"Do you think the killer meant for the body to be found?" said Arthur, as they meandered back down the sloping woods, taking a different path to their ascent in the hope of covering more potential truffle ground.

"It is possible. But perhaps Monsieur Ollie was only to be found after a time. Consider, it is likely he was shot on the Saturday, when Madame Eldridge saw him the last time. But the body was hidden, perhaps in hope that the rain would wash away some clues."

"Then what about the break-in on Monday?"

"Ah. Now that confuses me. Why does the murderer, if it is he, wait until Monday evening to break in to steal the map? What if Monsieur Ollie had been found before?"

"Tricky one. Maybe the murderer didn't twig about the map until later?"

"That assumes, *mon ami*, a particularly unintelligent murderer."

"Not every criminal can be an evil mastermind."

"That is true," said Chef Maurice, nodding. "Still, this map, it is a puzzle. Why did he not steal the map on the Friday before, at the first break-in?"

Arthur rubbed his forehead. "Maybe it wasn't the same person, then."

Chef Maurice gave him a condescending look. "Two burglaries in the one week? That is most unlikely."

They arrived back at the car. Truffles found: nil. Dead bodies: likewise. The pensioners had decamped to their cars for mid-morning packed lunches and, from the general level of chatter, they hadn't fared much better in their search.

Horace heaved himself into the back seat and keeled over for a long-overdue snooze. Hamilton sat in his basket, head hung, embarrassed to have failed once again in his truffle-hunting duties.

"Do not worry, *mon petit*," said Chef Maurice, patting him on the head. He produced a handful of sow nuts, which Hamilton gobbled up. "This afternoon, we will go to look for a map. Then the truffles, they will hide from us no more."

Laithwaites Manor occupied the crest of a small grassy hill over on the other side of Farnley Woods. The gravel crunched genteelly as Arthur rolled his Aston Martin up the wide drive. Hamilton, perched on Chef Maurice's lap, stuck his snout against the window and stared.

"Handsome old pile, isn't it?" said Arthur.

Chef Maurice regarded the manor, which was built from huge slabs of pale limestone, with tall sash windows and a majestic entrance flanked by columns.

"Cold," he replied. "The stone buildings, they are too cold."

"Le Cochon's a stone cottage, isn't it?"

"*Exactement*. I know the cold of stone. Why do you think we serve the twenty-four-hour roast lamb?"

Chef Maurice's bedroom was above the kitchens and, through trial and error, over the years he had managed to manoeuvre his bed to the spot directly over the ovens.

"Well, that explains a lot. I did always think you had an excessive amount of flambéed items on your winter menu."

Chef Maurice nodded. Dorothy might complain about the odd burning napkin incident, but you couldn't deny that flambéed sauces, pancakes and other desserts added theatre to the dining room, in addition to keeping the heating bill down.

They pulled on the bell pull. After a while, the old oak door swung back to reveal, in place of the creaky old butler Chef Maurice had half-expected, Brenda Laithwaites herself, chicly attired in well-pressed trousers, a cream silk blouse and a soft cardigan thrown over her shoulders.

"*Bonjour*, Madame Laithwaites. Do you enjoy lemons?" Chef Maurice proffered the *tarte au citron* that he'd liberated earlier from the restaurant's pantry.

"Oh, how lovely! And please, do call me Brenda. And Arthur too, how delightful to see you! Do come in."

Up close, Chef Maurice noticed that Brenda was wearing rather more make-up and perfume than he felt entirely comfortable with. There had also been the slight inflection in her voice on the phone that had him wondering if there was a Mr Laithwaites. Still, he hoped she hadn't misread his reasons for paying a visit; his intentions were of a strictly cartographical nature.

"What a little darling!" said Brenda, scooping Hamilton up

into her arms. So far starved of female attention, he nuzzled her elbows and squeaked contentedly. "Shall we go along to the kitchen? Let's find this little cutie something to eat."

"Your phone call was most opportune, *madame*," said Chef Maurice as she led them through a gloomy, maroon-carpeted hall. "We were intending to call you just today, in fact."

Above them, various stuffed animal heads hung from the walls. The collection included the obligatory constipated-looking moose, as well as a cross-eyed tiger and a trio of bears in descending size order.

"My grandfather was quite the big game hunter," said Brenda, following their gazes. "Though he nearly lost his arm to that chap up there." She pointed to a shaggy lion on the far wall.

"Do you hunt?" said Arthur, searching for something polite to say about the monstrosities above them. "I hear there are some good pheasant grounds near here."

Brenda shook her head. "That gene didn't pass my way, I'm afraid. Can't stand the noise those big guns make. Frankly, I'd sell off these awful specimens, except they're one of the few things we have left to remember Grandfather by."

The manor kitchen was smaller than Chef Maurice had envisaged, given the sprawling size of the building itself. The floor was tiled in squares of alternate black and white, spotlessly mopped, and the appliances, while not new, had clearly been carefully maintained and shone with elbow grease. He nodded approvingly.

They left Hamilton with a bowl of pre-chopped carrots and apples, watched over suspiciously by Missy the poodle, and followed Brenda in the direction of the private library. On the way, they passed several imposing oak doors, which, judging by the dust on the floor and door handles, hadn't been touched for some time.

The library, in contrast, was a light, high-ceilinged room with an impressive view over the lawns at the back of the house. Leather-bound books from bygone eras, spines worn with age, lined the walls and tall cabinets. In the corner, a smaller bookcase held a few rows of pastel-coloured novels, of the soppy sort that Dorothy pretended not to read during the occasional lull in service. There was also a small collection of cookbooks, though whoever had been purchasing them had stopped doing so sometime during the era of the Black Forest gâteau.

"Magnificent," said Arthur, roaming the shelves with the dreamy look of a true booklover.

"So kind of you to say," said Brenda, fussing with a bunch of lilies on the central table. "It's one of the few rooms I still keep open. Maintaining this old place costs a small fortune, just to keep it from crumbling. Still, we manage. Always have, always will, I'm sure."

Chef Maurice noticed an electric guitar, an expensive one by the looks of it, on a stand by the window. Next to all the books and the plump leather armchairs, it looked somewhat out of place. He reached over and plucked a string; it rang out dull and faded quickly.

"You are musical, *madame*?"

Brenda turned around and smiled fondly at the guitar. "It's Peter's, my son's. It's just him and me now, since Henry passed away five years ago."

Ah, so no Mr Laithwaites. Chef Maurice inched further out of the perfume radius and endeavoured to look less charming.

"It must be a comfort to have your son so close."

"When he's not holed up in his room," said Brenda with a smile. "He's off gallivanting with his friends in Spain at the moment. That's young people for you nowadays, globetrotters by the age of eighteen. He's seen more of the world than I have."

Arthur had now migrated over to the tall windows and was peering out at the checkerboard lawn and harmoniously spaced flowerbeds and shrubbery.

"I'm afraid I can't take credit for all this," said Brenda, stepping up beside him. "My father was simply mad about gardening. This was all his. I mean, he had help back in those days—I remember one point when we had three full-time garden staff, just to keep things tidy. He just loved to see things grow. He's the one who planted the apple and plum orchards round the west side of the house too."

Chef Maurice's ears pricked up. A free supply of apples and plums was not something to be sneezed at.

Brenda pointed at the tall treetops in the distance, the leaves now just turning golden. "You can just about see Farnley Woods from here." She paused. "I suppose you heard about the shooting?"

"Yes, we did," said Arthur quickly, before Chef Maurice could launch into a no-doubt-dramatic retelling. "Tragic, really."

"The police came round earlier, asking me if I'd heard anything. Not a peep, I told them." She shook her head. "Horrible business. Though I suppose poaching comes with its own dangers."

"He was a forager, *madame*."

"Poaching, foraging—it's all the same, isn't it?"

Chef Maurice and Arthur were too polite to correct her.

"Guns, honestly," she continued, "they're such horrible, dangerous things. But enough about that. You came to see me about the maps, didn't you?"

She walked over to the shelves and pulled down a large leather-bound portfolio. Little puffs of dust rose up as she laid it on the big mahogany table and flipped it open.

"Now, here's a map of the region from the eighteenth century. See how small Cowton was back in those days? And Farnley Woods was even bigger than it is now." She turned a few crackly pages. "Here's the Laithwaites Manor estate back in the 1920s. We owned a lot more land back in those days. See there"—she pointed to some faint lines— "that's the part of Farnley Woods that used to be part of the estate. My father had to sell it off in the sixties to pay for the upkeep of the rest of this place. Nearly broke his heart."

"These maps, they are expensive?" asked Chef Maurice, leaning in for a closer look.

"The older ones, maybe," said Brenda, turning another page. "To the right collector. But I had them valued a few years ago, and it hardly seemed worth the effort to try and sell them. In fact, they told me the more recent ones, the ones from the mid-1900s, they're just prints. I don't know where the originals are, or if we even owned them."

"Still, they're a fascinating slice of history," said Arthur, running a finger along the cracked leather.

"I'm glad you like them." Brenda smiled. "I'll just go see if the kettle's boiled. Take your time with these."

Chef Maurice carefully lifted another page over and frowned. All these maps appeared to be more concerned with land boundaries than botanical detail. Here and there, a squiggly marking suggested that trees might figure somewhere in it all, but there was no suggestion of what varieties, or the underlying soil types, let alone any mention of their truffle-producing potential.

"Hmmm, tough luck, old chap," said Arthur, who'd come to the same conclusion. "Maybe we've been barking up the wrong tree. There's no proof Ollie found those truffles near here. He might have brought them in from Italy, trying to pass them off as English truffles, for some kind of rarity value. You know what he was like."

Chef Maurice tapped his nose. "This, it does not lie. And also, why did Monsieur Ollie acquire a dog, if the truffles are not from here? I do not remember a dog last year."

"Maybe he got lonely."

"Bah! Then he should get a wife, not a dog."

"I think you'll find that wives," said Arthur, with utter certainty, "are much more trouble than dogs."

Chef Maurice shrugged. He'd never been particularly inclined to acquire either. Cheffing was a more-than-full-time commitment.

He turned another yellowed page.

"Wait, go back!" said Arthur. He flipped the page over and pointed to the corner of the map, which bore the description: *Civil Parish of Farnley and Woodlands Thereof, 1957.*

"Civil Parish of Farnley, 1957," said Arthur, voice lowered. "Remember that scrap from the corkboard? I'll bet you this is the same map Ollie had."

"But it is merely a print," said Chef Maurice. He ran a thick finger over the map. It was much the same as the one from the 1920s, showing the minuscule little squares of the Farnley cottages, as well as the main woodlands and the carefully demarcated estates of Laithwaites Manor and nearby Crinklewood Lodge. "Madame Brenda said it had no value. And it shows us nothing of interest."

"But remember what Mrs Eldridge said? Ollie had been drawing on the map. Maybe he had worked out—"

Whatever Ollie might have done was cut off by a piercing scream from the other end of the house and the sound of crashing crockery. It wasn't quite loud enough to curdle the blood, but it definitely set their pulses hammering.

Then another scream—this time higher, longer and squeakier.

It sounded like Hamilton.

CHAPTER 10

Patrick sat next to the telephone in the empty dining room of Le Cochon Rouge and stared at the card in his hand.

He prided himself on possessing a sound, logical mind. While cooking was a craft, and possibly even an art, it was definitely a science too. An egg didn't boil because it felt inspired. It was all down to protein molecules and chemical bonds. Easy stuff.

What wasn't so easy to understand was the card now in his hand. *Call me if you think of anything else*, she'd said.

And he had. He'd thought about how very nice it would be to ask her out on a date. Not the actual asking as such—his stomach was rapidly turning into concrete at the very thought. But going on a date, now that would be very nice indeed.

PC Lucy wasn't exactly beautiful—her nose was a little too sharp, her mouth a tiny bit too wide—but she came damn close in Patrick's opinion. There was something about her eyes, and the specks on her nose that hinted of summertime freckles, and the way her lips parted when she was deciding whether or not to start yelling at someone.

He'd never quite understood the term 'girl next door', seeing as when he was growing up the girl who lived next door had been several years older than him, and had once spent an afternoon shooting stones at him and his frog-breeding experiment (to wit, one pond, lots of frogs, and a clipboard).

But he definitely wouldn't have minded living next to PC Lucy.

So logically, there was no problem, then. She'd said he could call her if he thought of anything, and he had. He did have an inkling that there might be something wrong with this train of thought, but inklings weren't logical.

So he took a deep breath, picked up the phone and dialled.

After the third ring, it occurred to him that it might have been better to have first worked out what he was going to say.

"PC Gavistone here. Hello?"

Patrick's tongue was suddenly dry as a bag of bread-crumbs.

"Hello?" She sounded impatient.

"Er, hi. It's Patrick here. Um . . . "

"Patrick? Oh, yes. What can I do for you? Are you calling about the Meadows case?"

He could hear the buzz of an office in the background. She must be down at the Cowton police station.

"Not exactly. I was thinking, if it wasn't completely inappropriate, and of course it's totally fine if you say no, don't worry, I won't stalk you like a serial killer or something—"

Patrick's ears caught up with his tongue and sent a message to his brain that it might be a good idea to consider moving to Australia. Or New Zealand. Anywhere far enough from this conversation and the soon-to-be-issued restraining order.

"—um, sorry, I didn't mean it like that, just a joke. What I meant was, um, I was wondering . . . ifyou'dliketogo outtodinnerwithmesometime?"

"Sorry?" She sounded genuinely confused. "I didn't quite catch that."

"If you'd like to go out . . . to dinner . . . with . . . me?"

Silence reigned.

"Um." PC Lucy's voice sounded strangled. Was it with anger, laughter or sudden serial-killer-induced fear? "Can you give me a moment?"

The line went on hold.

Patrick glanced out the front dining room window. He wondered how long it would take for the car to arrive to arrest him for Propositioning an Officer of the Law.

He also wondered if kangaroo meat was any good for grilling. Perhaps with a little olive oil and a chilli-herb rub . . .

After what seemed like an eternity, the line clicked back on.

"That sounds great!" She sounded out of breath, and her words tumbled out. "How about tomorrow evening? My place? I'll c—" There was a muffled sound, like a hand on the receiver, and some incoherent shouting.

"Sorry about that," she said, after a moment.

"Um, no problem. You were saying?"

"Oh yes, dinner tomorrow. I'll cook," she said brightly.

"Really?" He couldn't help himself. "Oh. That's, um, great. I'll . . . see you then, then? Tomorrow evening, right?"

"Right."

The line went dead.

Patrick stared at the phone, then hung up. He stood up and walked back to the kitchen, his knees a little wobbly.

He'd just asked a girl out, and she'd said yes. She'd even offered to cook him dinner. That had never happened before.

He was halfway back to the kitchen when he was struck by a truly dreadful thought.

PC Lucy put the phone down and stared at the piece of scribbled paper in her hand.

"'I'll cook'? What the heck were you thinking?" She waved the paper in the face of PC Sara Shotter, who was sat on the edge of PC Lucy's desk, smirking.

"More than you were, when you hung up on the poor guy and I had to step in to save the day."

"I didn't hang up. I put him on hold."

"Sure. Because *that's* normal."

"I needed a moment to think."

PC Sara snorted. "If you'd been thinking any longer,

I'd have had to start drawing my pension. And look, now you've got a date. Which," she added, as PC Lucy opened her mouth to argue, "is a good thing."

"You say that like I never go on dates."

"You don't. And you need to, else you're going to fall into that whole bitter single female cop routine. And then there'll be nothing left for me to do except to enrol you in a beauty pageant so you can meet the man of your dreams." She paused. "Is it me, or does that film make no sense whatsoever?"

"Well, thankfully, we don't have beauty pageants around here."

"Uh-uh, we do," said PC Sara. "I saw a sign the other day for the annual Miss Clover competition."

"That's for cows, Sara. It's the annual Cowton livestock show."

"Seriously? You country folk are weird."

Sara had grown up in inner-city London, and therefore assumed all the idiosyncrasies encountered in her new countryside life were due to the effect of an overabundance of fresh air on the local population. By dint of her being the only other female officer in the team and about the same age as PC Lucy, they'd soon become de facto best friends.

"And since when do I invite strange men round to my flat and offer to cook them dinner? He's a *chef*, for goodness' sake! What am I going to make?"

"He's a chef?"

"Yes!"

"Ah. That could be a problem." PC Sara tapped a biro against her lip.

"You think?"

"How was I meant to know? You just said he was cute."

"No, I didn't!"

"Your tone of voice implied it."

PC Lucy glared at her.

"Why don't you serve oysters? I hear they're good on a date."

"We're landlocked around here, Sara. And I can't afford oysters."

"Roast a joint of meat? Leg of lamb? Men like a nice big lump of meat."

PC Lucy pictured the intricately crafted plates of food that issued from the kitchens of Le Cochon Rouge, each one of them a little work of art.

"I'm not sure if that's true for this one."

"Gavistone!" Chief Inspector Grant waved her over. "Enough chit-chat. Get over to this address here. There's been a reported kidnapping. Some French fella phoned it in. Kept repeating your name."

Uh-oh.

"It wasn't Mr Manchot, was it?"

"Something like that. Sounded like he'd swallowed a bucket of frogs. Anyway, off you go."

"I'll bring you in some cookbooks tomorrow," called Sara, as PC Lucy hurried out of the office.

A murder, and now a kidnapping. PC Lucy shook her head. It'd be arson next.

That, or just her setting fire to her flat trying to roast a chicken.

Arthur felt sorry for PC Lucy, as he watched her attempt to piece together a coherent version of the afternoon's events. It was hard to tell who was more hysterical: Brenda Laithwaites or Chef Maurice.

The chef kept jumping to his feet and pacing around the kitchen, firing questions at poor old Brenda, who was sat clutching Missy in her arms, red-faced and teary-eyed.

"How can it be! This man, he just runs in here and you do nothing?" Chef Maurice threw his hands in the air. "Poor Hamilton, he is a poor little *cochon*, he cannot defend himself from—"

"Remember, the man had a gun, Mr Manchot," said PC Lucy, who was sitting at the end of the table, looking like she could do with something much stronger than the camomile tea currently on offer.

"It is *déplorable*! To kidnap a poor defenceless animal! When will he be found?"

"Mr Manchot, please can you sit down a moment while—"

"Will there be, how do you say, a line-up? I insist to be there!"

"Mr Manchot, you weren't even in the room. And we don't do line-ups—"

"Bah!" He threw himself down into a chair and cut a savage slice out of the walnut-and-coffee-bean cake on the table. "The police in this country . . . " he muttered through a mouthful of crumbs.

PC Lucy drew a deep breath. "Mrs Laithwaites. You were in the middle of describing your assailant . . . ?"

Brenda screwed up her eyes in thought. "He was tall, quite wide in the shoulders, wearing a blue jumper."

"Do you remember anything else? Hair colour? Approximate age?"

"He was wearing one of those masks, the kind you wear when you go skiing."

"A balaclava?"

Brenda nodded. "It was black."

"A tall man? In a mask? Bah, that could be anyone!" said Chef Maurice, sawing off another slice.

"Apart from a short woman," said Arthur cheerfully, then regretted it as three pairs of baleful eyes bored into him.

"Mr Manchot, can you think of any reason someone would want to steal—"

"—pignap—"

"—pignap your micro-pig? Is he a valuable animal?"

Chef Maurice paused mid-chew. "There was a lady, yesterday. She did not have a nice look. I would think it is possible she is involved." He proceeded to outline the tale of Mrs Carter-Wright and the dreaded pig-walking-licence forms.

PC Lucy made a show of noting this down. "Anyone else? What about his previous owners?"

"The animal home, they said they had no records. He was found in the woods, they said."

PC Lucy turned back to Mrs Laithwaites.

"You said the intruder came and left through the external kitchen door, which wasn't locked?"

Brenda nodded. "I always unlock it in the mornings, in case Missy wants to go out."

"Did you notice anything going on outside? I mean, before the intruder entered?"

"I did think I heard a car earlier, but I wasn't expecting any more visitors, and we're so far from the road up here, I thought I must have just been imagining it . . . "

"Bah!" muttered Chef Maurice.

Arthur got up and peered out of the kitchen door into the gravelled side path.

"Can't see much of the road from up here," he reported. "You can see a bit of the cars through the trees, but I doubt anyone driving by could properly see the side of the house, I'm afraid."

"You can't see the front either. The trees on the driveway completely cover the road," said PC Lucy, scribbling in her notebook. "Still, I'll see if there have been any reports of suspicious cars loitering in the area. I don't suppose there are any security cameras monitoring the grounds?"

"No," said Brenda ruefully. "I've been meaning to get some installed, but I've always felt quite safe here. Especially with Missy around."

"Hmph!" said Chef Maurice. "The dog, it did not even

bark. We found it hiding in a cupboard!"

Missy had the decency to bury her nose in Brenda's cardigan.

"Well, I think that covers it all," said PC Lucy, closing her notebook. "Will you be all right here alone?" she added to Mrs Laithwaites.

"Oh, don't worry about me. I'll be fine. My son Peter will be back from holidays this evening. I'll tell him to get a taxi home from the station. I don't quite feel like driving at this moment."

"Totally understandable," said Arthur.

Brenda turned to him and Chef Maurice. "I'm so sorry this happened here. If there's anything I can do . . . "

"Don't be ridiculous," said Arthur gallantly, as Chef Maurice continued to glare at Missy. "There's nothing you could have done, and thank the heavens you weren't hurt."

Brenda looked relieved.

After the necessary goodbyes, the front door clicked shut behind them, and they heard a bolt scrape into place.

"Mr Manchot, can I have a quick word in private?" said PC Lucy, drawing the chef aside.

"Of course, *mademoiselle*."

They both looked at Arthur.

"I'll go warm up the car, shall I?" he said.

Chef Maurice and PC Lucy wandered off round the corner of the building. A few minutes later, they reappeared, PC Lucy writing something in her notebook.

"The education of the young people in England, it is extremely lacking," said Chef Maurice as he climbed in next to Arthur.

"Come on, now, she's doing a fine job as it is."

"Eh? *Non*, not the police . . . "—he waved his hands—" . . . things. Mademoiselle Lucy, she asks me how to roast a chicken! *Incroyable!* What do they teach in the schools?"

Arthur shrugged. "Trigonometry and Latin, it was in my day. Back to Beakley?"

Chef Maurice stared morosely out of the window.

"I'm sure Hamilton will turn up soon, right as rain," said Arthur, as they swung out of the drive. "It might all turn out to be some elaborate practical joke."

In truth, he wasn't even convincing himself, but what else was there to be said in such a situation?

"Anyway, let's go get some lunch. I'm driving up to Gloucestershire this afternoon for an interview. You should come along, take your mind off things. I think you'd be rather interested in meeting this particular lady . . . "

Hamilton was not a happy pig.

It had all been going so well. The nice lady who smelled like flowers had given him a big bowl of apples and carrots. He liked apples and carrots.

Then there'd been a bang at the door, and a tall human had rushed in and thrown a sack over him. He'd cried for help, but to no avail.

Now here he was in a big cardboard box, watching the

ceiling bob up and down as someone carried him up what felt like a long flight of stairs.

Then hands reached down and grabbed him by the middle—he tried to bite, but ended up with a snoutful of woolly jumper—and now he found himself in a bigger box, this time a crate lined with hay. A single lightbulb buzzed high up above.

There was a musty smell in the air. It smelt of human sweat, ancient dust, and an odd whiff of lavender.

In fact, it all smelt rather . . .

. . . familiar.

CHAPTER 11

Miss Fey's cottage was hidden down the end of a narrow, windy lane, nestled in the dense woodlands that spread for miles in all directions. Thick ivy crept across the whole front wall, giving the cottage the look of a boxy hedge with windows, and autumn berries hung from the low thatched roof.

The smell of apricot pie wafted out of the open window, and Chef Maurice found himself cheering up, despite recent events. Until he could find out more about Hamilton's disappearance, it would be impossible to mount a rescue mission. He would just need to bide his time, and accost any blue-jumper-clad balaclava-wearing men he met in the interim.

"Whatever you do, don't insult her or her produce," said Arthur, as they pulled up in front of the cottage.

"*Mon ami*, I would never—"

"And don't get me involved in your negotiations. In fact, keep the negotiations until after the interview. No haggling over the price of cèpes the minute we get in there, understand?"

"*Oui, oui*, I will sit in the corner like a good English schoolboy."

Arthur shot him a dubious look.

A hand-painted sign over the door announced: *Miss Fey's Wild Mushrooms. Hand-picked with love and care. Wholesale prices available, ask inside.*

In smaller writing below: *No dogs, no salesmen, no TV chefs.*

Arthur's knock was answered with a speed that suggested the door's owner had been lurking behind it the whole time. Miss Fey, though small in stature, had the kind of tough, desiccated look that told any onlookers that neither sleet nor snow nor nuclear warheads would get in her way. Her face was nut-brown from many summers spent outdoors and she wore her hair in a long white plait.

She eyed them through the wedge of open door, then flung it open and stuck out a gnarled hand.

"You must be that newspaper chappy," she said. "I'm Miss Fey. That's Miss with an eye and two esses. None of this mumbly Ms nonsense, got that?"

"Completely," said Arthur. "And thank you for agreeing to this interview. This is a friend of mine—"

"You're that chef from that little place down in Beakley," said Miss Fey, her beady eyes roaming across Chef Maurice's face. "I came visiting a few years ago, you might remember, but you said you already had a mushroom supplier. Not so much the case now, eh?"

Her eyes glinted as she watched for their reaction.

"Ah, it is good to see you again," lied Chef Maurice, who had the memory of a Nobel Prize winner when it came to food, but the recall ability of a distracted goldfish when it came to names and faces. "So I see you have heard the sad tale of Monsieur Ollie?"

"Sad tale? Codswallop. He got what was coming to him in my opinion. Nasty piece of work, that boy was."

"He was?" said Arthur, who was a perennial Believer in People.

"Dyed in the wool. Tricked me out of my best morel patch last year. Must have been following me, the little thief—not a chance he'd have found it himself. Picked the whole lot clean out after I left. Didn't even leave the small ones, and bad business, that is. Mushroom picking ain't a snatch-and-go. You've got to respect the woods. That boy, he had no respect."

"So you were not a friend of his, *madame*."

"Hah, you can say that. Then again, not many were. Oh, he had his lady friends, quite a number I heard, but when push came to shove . . . no, that boy didn't have many friends. Enemies, now, that's another matter."

She left this pronouncement hanging tantalisingly in the air, then clapped her hands together. "Right, enough speaking ill of them that deserves it. You wanted to learn about mushrooms, didn't you?" She darted inside and re-appeared in a wool jacket and broad-brimmed hat, carrying a large empty basket. "Then let's go."

Chef Maurice saw Arthur glance down at his spotless

leather brogues with a look of dismay. The chef himself was wearing his usual steel-capped boots, which the manufacturers claimed were oil-proof, flame-proof, blade-proof, and capable of withstanding the pressure of a tap-dancing elephant in stilettos. A little mud wasn't going to do them any harm.

They struck out eastwards, with Miss Fey leading the way.

"See here, this is your winter chanterelle," she said, bending down to pluck up an orange-brown specimen. "They love sweet chestnut trees. Find a good tree and every year you'll find them in exactly the same spot." She patted the tree next to her. "People think it's all about eyes to the ground, but it's actually all about the trees. This wood is like an old friend. Know your trees, and you'll know your mushrooms."

She stooped down again and plucked up another mushroom, almost identical to the first.

"Now this one"—she held out the new mushroom in her hand—"might look a lot like our first one. But see the gills here?" She flipped it over. "The true winter chanterelle has forked ridges. This one doesn't. We call them false chanterelles. Dangerous little things, can put you in hospital for a week."

"A risky business," murmured Arthur, making notes.

Miss Fey turned her sharp eyes on him. "You don't know the half of it."

"What is this one?" asked Chef Maurice, squatting down next to a small ring of spindly grey mushrooms with dull brown caps.

"Those are your liberty caps. Eat those, and you'll be seeing dancing pink giraffes for three days. They call them magic, but can't see what's so magic about them myself. They're a Class A drug nowadays, they'll lock you up for life if they catch you with them."

Chef Maurice withdrew his hand.

"Worth much, are they?" asked Arthur.

"Not enough to be worth the trouble to most people," said Miss Fey. "Not that you'd catch me touching those things for any sum of money. Law's there for a reason, I always say."

Chef Maurice cocked his head. There was something in the way she'd said it . . .

"There are other pickers, perhaps, who think different?"

She gave him an appraising look. "Might be. You hear a thing or two. Us pickers, we always have an ear to the ground, so to speak."

"But it would not do to speak ill of the dead, *n'est-ce pas*?"

Miss Fey gave him a humourless smile. "You ask a lot of questions, Mr Maurice. You're not Belgian, are you?"

"I am French, *madame*."

"Is that so? I knew a Belgian once, a little fellow. He asked a lot of questions too."

After another twenty minutes of poking around in the leaf mould, Foraging 101 was deemed complete and they retired to Miss Fey's cosy front room, which reeked of dried mushrooms and old books. Chef Maurice wandered up and down the bookshelves as Miss Fey clattered about in the kitchen.

The Handy Hedgerow Guide. Tales from the Deep Woods. The Nettle: Rituals, Remedies and Rhymes.

From up in the far corner, he pulled down a thin red volume titled: *Annals of European Mycology and Biotechnology, Vol. XIX.*

The text was small and dense, written by serious people who knew serious stuff, such as how to deploy a footnote to devastating effect.

Chef Maurice shut the book and placed it carefully back on the shelf.

"Milk, sugar, gentlemen?"

Their host reappeared with a tray laden with a blue-and-white china tea set, a steaming apricot pie and generous slices of lemon poppy seed cake.

"Milk and three sugars," said Chef Maurice automatically. He then noticed the size of the sugar cube in her dainty tongs. "And two more sugars. *Merci.*"

They settled back into the well-worn chintz armchairs.

Chef Maurice sought around for a suitable teatime topic.

"I wonder, *madame*, if you are familiar with the English truffle?"

The cake knife clattered off the tray and hit the rug.

"Deary me, excuse my butter fingers," said Miss Fey, putting on her glasses and bending down to retrieve the knife. "You were saying— Oh yes, English truffles. Poor specimens, I'll say, when you think about what you can find elsewhere. We get the summer truffle in some parts, and I've heard rumours of a few patches of Burgundy truffles, but those who know of them keep their lips tight, as you can imagine."

"But none of the black Périgord? And the white truffle of Alba?"

She gave him a steady look from over her spectacles. "I do hope someone hasn't been pulling your leg, Mr Maurice. We don't have any of the likes of them in these parts." She stirred her tea slowly. "I'd know, believe me."

And that was the end of that conversational vein.

Arthur moved into interview mode, pen poised, while Chef Maurice decided to investigate the maximum of pie and cake that could fit onto a single small plate.

Even so, he kept one eye on Miss Fey, though this resulted in a certain amount of crumb fallout in the process.

As they left, she presented them each with a basket of fresh wild mushrooms. Chef Maurice, in line with his own expectations, got the bigger one.

"My number's on the card there," said Miss Fey, tucking it in behind a pile of white puffballs. "Should you be needing a new supplier at some point . . . "

"What a nice lady," said Arthur as he manoeuvred the car back down the lane.

"Mmmm." Chef Maurice looked over his shoulder at

the cottage as they pulled round a bend, just in time to see a curtain twitch shut.

He had the distinct feeling there was more than met the eye when it came to Miss Fey.

They spent the rest of the afternoon driving around the roads surrounding Laithwaites Manor with the windows rolled down, shouting Hamilton's name.

At least, Chef Maurice did. Arthur pulled his hat lower down on his forehead and crossed his fingers that Brenda's neighbours weren't the trigger-happy hunting types.

Eventually, no micro-pigs forthcoming, they drove in silence back to Le Cochon Rouge, Chef Maurice soothing his raw throat with a dose of medicinal cognac.

In the kitchens, dinner prep was underway. Patrick looked up from julienning a stack of leeks.

"A cool box arrived with your name on it, chef. Marked private. I put it in the walk-in."

It was a small polystyrene container, about the size of a shoebox. Scrawled across the top was the message, *For Mr Manchot. PRIVATE.*

Chef Maurice levered the box open with a long spatula.

(Ever since the incident with a particularly truculent crab, this had been the official Cochon Rouge policy on opening mysterious packages. Alf still claimed to have the occasional nightmare about crustaceans.)

Inside, he found a handwritten note.

Keep your snout out of business that doesn't concern you, if you ever want to see your pig again.

Under the note was a shrink-wrapped packet of bacon.

CHAPTER 12

Chef Maurice jabbed at the frying pan with a wooden spoon. Sizzling fat spluttered onto the hob.

"You're not actually cooking that bacon, are you?"

Patrick kicked the mud off his boots in the kitchen doorway. Morning light filtered in through the small windows, and brown leaves jumped and swirled outside in the yard.

"And why should I not?"

"How can you be completely sure it's not . . . Hamilton?"

Chef Maurice lifted up a streaky brown rasher with his spoon. "It is much too large. And from the smell, I conclude this is from a British Saddleback pig."

"Still, I can't believe you're eating bacon today."

"But why not? My *grand-père*, he owned two horses, for the fields. And my *grand-mère* still made horsemeat stew every Sunday in the winter."

"Touching." Patrick poked his head into the walk-in fridge and noticed the basket Chef Maurice had returned with yesterday. "Are we putting these new mushrooms on the menu?"

"They are not enough," said Chef Maurice, assembling himself a bacon-and-egg sandwich between two thick slices of country loaf. "Instead, we will make sautéed wild mushrooms with tarragon and chives on sourdough bread for the staff meal. To test the quality, of course."

"Sounds good to me, chef. Um, do you know if Arthur is coming in for lunch today?"

Arthur had a standing lunch reservation every day at Le Cochon Rouge, and made use of it most days of the week when he was in Beakley and Meryl was out at work. On busy days when all other tables were booked out and they had to give away his table, he'd kick up a huge fuss, claiming to be their best and most loyal customer, then finally agree to eat standing in the kitchens.

"He did not say. What do you require of him?"

Patrick's ears reddened slightly. "I just needed to ask his advice about something . . . "

"Bah! A good chef never asks the advice of a food critic!"

"No, no, er, it wasn't about cooking. Um . . . "

Chef Maurice looked puzzled, then his eyes lit up. "Ah, then it must be about—"

"I printed out those flyers you wanted," said Patrick desperately, thrusting a stack of paper into Chef Maurice's hands.

"Ah, *très bien*! Most impressive!"

Chef Maurice had no love for modern technology, and to judge by the dents in the old battered desktop computer now collecting dust in his office, modern technology felt the same way about him.

Earlier in the year, Patrick's short-lived experiment with an online reservations system had ended abruptly when Chef Maurice leant his elbow on the keyboard and accidentally cancelled every reservation across the Valentine's Day weekend. This resulted in a severe overbooking of tables, and thus a string of highly disgruntled would-be paramours were forced to sit outside in the impromptu 'decking area', cobbled together from borrowed garden furniture and a few old picnic benches, while their dates stayed muffled up in their thick coats—not exactly the best scenario for fanning the flickering flames of a nascent romance.

Chef Maurice turned the flyer this way and that. "It is a good picture, *non?*"

It bore the missive: PIG MISSING. REWARD OFFERED. APPLY AT LE COCHON ROUGE.

Below was a grainy photo of Hamilton, taken by Dorothy on Hamilton's first day at the restaurant.

"What reward are we offering, chef?"

"That's depends," said Chef Maurice darkly, "on in what condition they find my pig."

"We could offer a three-course dinner for two here at the restaurant."

Chef Maurice liked that idea. It sounded suitably generous, while having the added benefit of his not having to withdraw any money from his actual bank account.

"Have you heard from Mademoiselle Lucy?"

Patrick looked up in panic. "What do you mean?"

"Eh? About the case, of course! My Hamilton! Have the police any developments?"

"What? How should I know? Why do you think I'd know anything?"

The two men looked at each other in mutual incomprehension.

"I go," said Chef Maurice finally, "to make a distribution of these papers."

Arthur had been oddly unwilling to demand a full-page ad from his editors at the England Observer, but offered to help pin up the notices all around Beakley and the nearby villages.

"No word yet from the police?"

"Pah! I telephone them. They say it is under control."

"Which could mean anything, I'm sure. Still, I suppose they do have a murder investigation going on, which I imagine takes precedence."

Chef Maurice hammered a flyer onto a nearby telegraph pole.

"Eh? You are saying that until they find the murderer of Monsieur Ollie, they will not look for Hamilton?"

"Well, you can hardly expect—"

"That is *intolérable*!" He paused. "Still, it gives me an idea . . . "

They continued their walk through the village, going door to door handing out flyers. Beakley's mostly retired residents could usually be depended upon to be at home, or visiting someone else's home, where they sat ready to pounce on the next visitor collecting for charity or selling double-glazing, dragging them in to dispense the latest gossip. They rarely bought anything—apart from the recent case of Mr Evans, who had been quite taken with the Avon lady, and whose newfound interest in rouge was said to be adding a whole new slant to his social life—but this didn't stop armies of salespeople making their regular rounds in Beakley, sure of a cup of tea and a slice of sponge cake.

Eventually they reached the end of the village and the cordoned-off cottage of Ollie Meadows, and found Mrs Eldridge sitting on a deck chair in her half of the front garden, a tartan blanket across her knees.

"Move out of my way, you're blocking the view," she snapped, waving at them with her cane. They obediently stepped aside and watched as Mrs Eldridge applied a pair of binoculars to her eyes and peered at the white van coming towards them. She pursed her lips, whipped on her reading glasses, and made a small entry in the notebook on her lap.

"Traffic control," she said, waving the little book at them. "I keep telling the council we need some traffic-calming devices in the village. The through traffic has been terrible of late."

Chef Maurice and Arthur turned to survey the empty road. In the distance, the van trundled off over a hill. Birds tweeted in the still trees.

"And what's that paper you've got there? I saw you both, plastering the whole village with those things."

They handed her a flyer, which she took and scrutinised as if it were the terms and conditions of a winning lottery ticket.

"So you've lost your pet pig, eh? My father used to keep pigs. They don't make good pets, I'll tell you that. Always getting loose and raiding the orchard next door, especially this time of year, when the fruit falls and rots on the ground. Turns to cider all by itself. You ever seen a drunk pig?"

They shook their heads.

"Ah, well, you're missing out, then."

"I have been threatened, Madame Eldridge," said Chef Maurice gravely. "They steal Hamilton, they tell me to stay out of Monsieur Ollie's business." This wasn't strictly accurate, but it seemed the most likely business that someone might want to keep him out of.

Mrs Eldridge nodded. "That Ollie had a lot of business that people might want to poke around into, if you get my meaning."

Arthur and Chef Maurice shared a look. This sounded promising.

"Have you, er, mentioned all this . . . business to the police?" said Arthur.

Mrs Eldridge snorted. "That pretty little blonde police lady wouldn't know a criminal if he hit her over the head. Kept me out of the house, she did, when they searched his cottage the other day. His half is a mirror image of mine. I could have told them all the places to look."

"Like, in the back of the wardrobes, under the stairs, below the sink, that kind of thing?"

Mrs Eldridge narrowed her eyes at Arthur. "You been having me watched?"

"Ahem," said Chef Maurice. "You were speaking of Monsieur Ollie and his business?"

"I might have been." Mrs Eldridge tilted her head. "But then again, I might have forgotten. My memory plays up something dreadful, it does."

Chef Maurice nodded. "I, myself, have that problem sometimes. But I think I have a remedy. Arthur, your phone, *s'il vous plaît*?"

Fifteen minutes later, the smell of caramelised pastry and slow-cooked apples filled Mrs Eldridge's little parlour room.

"Tell Patrick," Chef Maurice said to Alf, who was red in the face from his sprint down from Le Cochon Rouge, "that we will need another *tarte tatin* for dinner this evening."

"*Oui*, chef," said Alf, and jogged out of the door.

They sat, balancing their teacups on their knees.

"So first of all," said Mrs Eldridge, leaning forwards like one about to impart state secrets, "there's those youngsters that keep coming around."

"Local kids?" asked Arthur.

"Not from Beakley, else I'd know 'em by sight. They park up in the lay-by, near those fields behind here, and cut across through to the back." Mrs Eldridge waved her cane towards the rear of her house.

"What are they coming here for?"

"Ah, if I knew that, I might have bothered to tell that police lady. I know they come to pick up something, I see 'em scuttling away with paper bags sometimes."

"Do you see them exchanging anything?" asked Arthur. "Money and the like?"

"It's them darn eaves," said Mrs Eldridge, pointing her cane at the window. "Gets in the way when you're trying to look out. I can see the back path from my upstairs bedroom, but the way the eaves hang out, can't see what goes on at the door."

"A shame, *madame*," said Chef Maurice.

"Ain't it just? I wanted to put one of those little balconies on the back, but the council chap said I wasn't allowed, it'd be overlooking. I told him, young man, overlooking is exactly what I want it for!"

Chef Maurice made various sympathetic noises.

"But I wouldn't be bothering with those youngsters anyway," continued Mrs Eldridge. "Not if you're after something to do with Ollie's murder."

"Why do you say that, *madame*?" said Chef Maurice, helping himself to another slice of *tarte tatin*, and making a mental note to try adding a touch of cinnamon next time.

"Got my money on one of those two fellows who've been hanging around here."

"Fellows?" said Arthur.

"Well, the first one, saw him last Friday—"

"That is the day Monsieur Ollie's cottage was first broken into!" said Chef Maurice.

Mrs Eldridge nodded. "Saw him here a few times that day, bold as brass, staring through the windows, banging on the door. Reckon he waited until dark, then . . . well, just as well Ollie was out that night. Off with a lady friend, he was, by my reckoning."

"You think the murderer came for him that night?" said Arthur.

"It makes sense," said Chef Maurice. "Nothing was taken on the Friday. Perhaps because it was not the intention."

"You might be right about that," said Mrs Eldridge. "And I saw him again, the same man, on the Sunday afternoon. Shouted something through the letter box, then drove off."

"You have his car details?"

Mrs Eldridge tapped her notebook. "All in here."

"But that doesn't make sense," said Arthur, drumming his fingers on his knee. "Ollie had already . . . disappeared by then. Why come back to the cottage?"

"Aha, perhaps he returns to create an alibi?"

"Damn funny alibi. And then there's the break-in on Monday too. Why come back again, break in, and steal a worthless map? It doesn't make sense."

"Patience, *mon ami*. To solve a mystery, it is like clarifying the chicken stock. In time, it will become clear." He turned to Mrs Eldridge. "This man, what did he look like?"

Mrs Eldridge peered down at her notebook. "He was tall, not old, not young, a big man, looked like he could heave a crate or two."

"Hmm, the man I saw break in on the Monday night was a skinny chap," said Arthur.

"He had a big dark beard—"

"The dog man!" cried Chef Maurice. "*Mon ami*, this must be the same man who collected the dog of Monsieur Ollie."

"Our phantom truffle hunter?"

Chef Maurice nodded.

Mrs Eldridge, who sensed the limelight was fading away from her, rapped her pen against her notebook. "Then there's that second fellow who's been coming round."

"A skinny chap?" said Arthur hopefully.

She shook her head. "Big fellow. All dressed up, business-like. Blond hair. Tall."

"Hmph, all these criminals, always tall," muttered Chef Maurice.

"So what was suspicious about this chap, then?"

"Well, it was the Thursday night he came around. Ollie didn't want to let him in at first, then he did. I could hear them shouting through the walls. Terrible the way sound carries through these walls. Had to turn the telly right down, I did."

"What were they shouting about?"

"Well, it was mostly the blond fellow doing the shouting. Couldn't make out most of it. Something about staying away from something."

Chef Maurice thought about the note they'd found in Ollie's house. *Keep away from things that don't belong to you. Or else.*

"Not much to go on, I'm afraid," said Arthur. "Frankly, my money's on those kids and those packages. Drugs, most likely."

Chef Maurice frowned. PC Lucy hadn't mentioned finding any drugs. The good citizens of Beakley mostly confined themselves to the wholesomely legal highs of alcohol and gossip.

"What did these kids look like?" asked Arthur.

"Well, it wasn't always the same ones. There was one boy, though, saw him a lot, always wearing a black jacket. Fancied himself as James Dean, I reckon. Girls sometimes too, wearing those ridiculous shoes they do nowadays. They never caused any trouble, mind you," she added. "Except for the smoking. They'd stand out the back, waiting for Ollie. Like clockwork they was. Every Friday early evening, regular."

"Every Friday?" Chef Maurice looked at Arthur. "That is today. *Mon ami*, are you thinking what I am thinking?"

Arthur sighed. "I highly doubt it."

CHAPTER 13

They headed back to Le Cochon Rouge for lunch, plans thus arranged for later that afternoon. Arthur had fervent misgivings about the whole enterprise, but Chef Maurice was insistent: solving this murder was Hamilton's only chance.

They found Patrick pacing up and down the kitchens and muttering to himself, his hair sticking out at odd angles. This was unusual; as chefs went, Patrick was as well balanced as a tightrope-walking accountant's chequebook.

He had his eyes half-closed and was gesturing with one hand. "Delicious!" he muttered. "That was really . . . delicious . . . "

"I don't think he's quite got the vocabulary to be a restaurant critic," said Arthur, sotto voce, to Chef Maurice.

Chef Maurice wandered over to Alf, who was pushing a steaming pile of potatoes through a ricer.

"What is the matter with Patrick?"

"He's got a date. With a girl," said Alf with a smirk. "She's going to cook him dinner."

"Ah, jolly good," said Arthur. "So who's the lucky lady?"

"It's that blonde policewoman," said Alf. "Never knew Patrick had a thing for uniforms . . . "

Patrick stopped pacing and threw his hands open at his audience. "What am I going to *do*?"

They stared at him.

Arthur cleared his throat. "Exactly which part of the evening are you referring to?" he said carefully.

"She said she's going to cook! What if I don't like her cooking?"

Arthur looked sideways at the assembled company. Alf was still at the age where girls presented both a fascination and a terror *incognita*. As for Chef Maurice, while he could muster a certain brisk variety of charm when matters required, a prolonged but not unhappy bachelorhood had now led to the stage where an evening with a well-curated cheeseboard held more attraction to the chef than the perils of female companionship.

Which left Arthur, who, despite several years of joyous marriage, rather regarded this feat like a man who has accidentally solved a Rubik's Cube—he was damned if he knew how it all worked, let alone in a position to advise someone else on its mechanics.

"What if she's an awful cook? Should I lie?"

"Never," said Chef Maurice, who lied all the time.

"Absolutely," said Arthur, the happily married man. "Make sure to have second helpings too. The way to a woman's heart is through your stomach."

Patrick looked pained. "Can I at least offer constructive criticism?"

"Not if you don't want her to retaliate," said Arthur, patting him on the shoulder. "Especially at a point in the evening when you least expect it." He winced. "So when is this date?"

"Tonight." Patrick looked glum.

"Cheer up, she might turn out to be an excellent cook," said Arthur. He'd once seen PC Lucy judo-tackle a would-be bicycle thief on the village green. Pacifying a rack of lamb would surely be no trouble. That said, there had been that roast chicken question the other day . . .

"You could skip lunch," volunteered Alf. "That way you'll be raving hungry."

"And what are we even going to talk about?"

"Films, books, music? The joys of village life?" Arthur racked his brain. It had been many decades since he'd had to make ulteriorly motivated small talk.

"Whether she has found *mon* Hamilton?"

"*Not* that," said Arthur. "Keep work out of the equation."

As he headed for the dining room and his reserved lunchtime table, he heard Chef Maurice offer up one more tip from his personal dating philosophy.

"And do not forget to check her fridge. You can tell much about a lady by the cheese that she eats."

Bachelorhood, thought Arthur, was a strange world, indeed.

* * *

It would probably go down as one of history's best-catered stake-outs.

They sat in the lay-by in Chef Maurice's car—Arthur had taken one look at the overflowing picnic hamper and vetoed taking his Aston—surrounded by four types of cheese, two cold game pies, a roast artichoke quiche, a fruit platter, and an extra-large thermos of hot chocolate.

The late afternoon sun was just setting behind the trees. Over the ridge in front of them, unkempt fields led down the hill to the lower part of Beakley village and, in particular, to the back door of Ollie Meadows' old cottage.

"It's been an hour already," said Arthur, jiggling his knees. "Do you think she got the day wrong?"

"Madame Eldridge is a most conscientious lady."

Arthur tested his seat to see if it could go any lower. Not that it mattered too much—he was already confident that from the road, a casual passer-by could hardly see him.

Chef Maurice, on the other hand, had simply donned the large pork-pie hat that he saved for special occasions.

"It is a good disguise, *non*?" he said, noticing Arthur's stare.

Arthur was about to point out that, hat or no hat, it wasn't hard to recognise the only man in Beakley with a moustache large enough to warrant its own postcode, when a VW Beetle roared into the lay-by and pulled up in front of them.

135

Two girls in their late teens, who had apparently dressed in expectation of a day at the beach, rather than a chilly autumn evening, jumped out and tottered off down the slope.

Arthur and Chef Maurice scrambled out of the car and hurried over to the ridge. They could see the top of the girls' heads as they picked their way down the zigzag path towards the cottages.

"We must get close enough to observe their conversation," whispered Chef Maurice. He took a step forward and a branch cracked loudly underfoot.

"Quick! Get down!" He grabbed Arthur's leg and dragged him into the long grass.

"Ouch! Maurice, you really didn't have to—"

But Chef Maurice was already creeping away down the slope, bent double and using his hands as paddles to part a way through the grassy wilderness.

They could hear the girls' voices raised in complaint.

"—almost snapped my heel. Beats me why PJ makes us come round this way. It's not like there's much going on in this place."

"Ow, I think I've got a stone in my shoe. Yeah, well, he can come next week, now that he's back, and save us all this faff."

Arthur, concentrating on the conversation, almost tripped over Chef Maurice, who was lying flat on the ground in a small clearing in the grass. A few metres in front of him was a very plump brown rabbit. It twitched its nose at them.

"Come here, little *lapin*," whispered Chef Maurice, inching forward on his elbows, his hat raised in one hand.

"Maurice, what do you think you're—"

"Did you hear that?" One of the girls stopped walking.

"What?"

"I thought I heard something. Coming from over there?"

"You sure?"

There was a rustle as one of them took a tentative step into the tall grass.

Arthur gave Chef Maurice a 'what do we do now?' look.

Chef Maurice sighed, replaced his hat and picked up a nearby stick. He gave the rabbit a gentle prod in the direction of the voices.

The rabbit wrinkled its nose and gave him a reproachful look.

"I think I just saw something—"

"*Allez-y!*" whispered Chef Maurice, and gave the rabbit a harder prod. This time it took the hint, and lopped off in the direction of the cottages.

A few moments later, one of the girls squealed.

"Aww!"

"Just a rabbit," said the other.

"But isn't it cute?"

"Chrissy, come *on* . . . "

The girls finished their descent, adjusted their clothing and rapped on Ollie's back door.

No answer.

"What's all this yellow tape for?"

"Dunno, maybe he's doing building work?"

"Do you think he's forgotten we're coming?"

"He's not like that. Maybe PJ changed the day. Told you we should have called him when we landed."

"I told you, my phone's out of juice. What did you do with yours?"

"It's back at the bottom of the hotel pool— Don't look at me like that. It slipped."

"Funny how you managed to hold onto your tenth cocktail pretty fine. So what do we do now?"

"Let's go meet the others. Maybe PJ's already been and didn't tell us."

Bickering half-heartedly, the two girls traipsed back up the hill.

Arthur nudged Chef Maurice.

"Eh?"

Arthur stabbed his finger towards the lay-by, and made the frantic 'driving along holding the steering wheel' motion that people make when pretending to drive a car, and which would lead to severe pile-ups if they ever tried it in a real vehicle.

"Ah! A chase!"

"Shhh!"

They clambered back up the hill, taking a straight path through the overgrowth. Up ahead, there was the sound of slamming doors and wheels on gravel.

"Hurry up before we lose them!"

Arthur ran the rest of the way up the hill, his knees sending out fiery sparks of protest, and wrenched open the passenger door. He turned around, but Chef Maurice was nowhere to be seen.

"Maurice!"

Chef Maurice appeared, puffing, over the crest of the hill, carrying his upturned hat in both hands. In the hat sat a very plump brown rabbit, its feet upturned, twitching its nose at the surroundings.

"Maurice, come on! We're on a stake-out, not an animal rescue mission."

"I thought he would make a good friend for Hamilton."

"When we get Hamilton back, we can go get a rabbit. Now put that one back where you found it, heaven knows where it's been!"

There was the squeal of brakes as the girls' car reached the bottom of the hill.

"Get in the car!"

A moment later, after a precipitous U-turn that left Arthur clutching the dashboard with one hand and his stomach with the other, they were barrelling down the hill after the VW Beetle.

The chase was on.

CHAPTER 14

PC Lucy surveyed her troops. Two large onions. A bag of arborio rice. Chicken stock, shop-bought—but still, better than a stock cube, surely? A small wedge of parmesan, slivers of which she kept popping into her mouth. A large block of butter.

(She could hear her mother's voice, saying one could never have enough butter when it came to dinnertime. Witnesses to Mrs Gavistone's impressive bearing might have begged to differ.)

The gourmet food store in Cowton had only had one packet of dried mushrooms left on its shelves. PC Lucy snipped it open and tipped the whole lot into the pot. It didn't look like much. And the last thing she wanted was for Patrick to think she'd skimped on ingredients. Still, it would have to do. Unless . . .

Her gaze slid across the room to a large clear plastic box containing the various bags of dried mushrooms she'd removed from Ollie's lodgings, if only for the purpose of stopping Chef Maurice from getting at them. She'd been meaning to lug the box down to the station, though frankly the evidence room—which also served as the broom cupboard—was full enough as it was.

No. It would probably be unprofessional to start cooking the evidence from a murder case. She'd just have to manage with what she had.

Sara had written down her mother's supposedly famous recipe for mushroom risotto.

"Isn't your mum from Skegness?"

"So?"

PC Lucy had stared at the recipe. She was no culinary wizard, but she was fairly sure that risotto wasn't usually made with beef suet. Nor was it fried. Or served with gravy.

So she'd had to make do with a recipe she'd found on the Internet. Forty-eight people had 'liked' it and there were only two complaints, one of which pointed out sniffily that the recipe was a little heavy on the carbs.

Still, there was one secret weapon in her arsenal, in the form of a heftily priced bottle of French wine that the man in the gourmet food shop had promised would set her dish dancing on the palate. If Patrick liked wine even half as much as his boss did, hopefully she was in with a chance that he'd be sloshed enough to not notice her cooking too much . . .

She stuck a spoon into the cloggy mess at the bottom of the pot. It tasted like two-day-old rice pudding.

In desperation, she threw in the last wodge of parmesan, which just sat there, sinking slowly like a cheesy Titanic.

She wondered if Chef Maurice would still let her eat at Le Cochon Rouge after she served his sous-chef a dish of congealed cheese-and-rice-based sludge.

Her gaze wandered again to the box of concentrated mushroomy goodness sitting in the corner.

Surely no one would notice if just a handful went missing.

She lifted up the lid and the deep meaty fragrance of wild mushrooms hit her nostrils.

Just one handful. What harm could it do . . . ?

There are certain conventions best adhered to when one is tailing another vehicle. There's the surreptitious hanging back, maintaining a safe twenty metres' distance between you and your prey. In busy traffic, best to leave at least three cars as a buffer zone, just in case. Inconspicuous attire is also recommended.

There should not, on the other hand, be any tailgating, horning at the targeted car when you think it's driving too slowly, nor subsequently trying to overtake when they don't take the hint.

"Maurice," said Arthur, gripping the side of the car as they took a hairpin bend at more than double the recommended speed, "I don't think you've grasped the fundamental concept of tailing someone. Namely, that you stay *behind*."

"But this way, they do not think we are following them."

"We *aren't* following them. We might have even lost them, there were a lot of turn-offs back there . . . "

He craned his neck to see out of the back windscreen. In the distance, the girls' car appeared round the bend.

"There they are. Pull over!"

"But they will—"

"Just pull over! And try to look inconspicuous."

"Bah!" But he pulled over nonetheless. A few moments later, the VW Beetle puttered past them.

"Right, after them!" said Arthur, straightening up from his ducked position. Chef Maurice threw aside the newspaper he'd been pretending to read and stomped on the accelerator.

They were approaching the northern edge of Cowton, Beakley's nearest large town and home to the country's smallest watchtower, an annual Goose Fair, and a particular type of local cider that dissolved your teeth and brain cells in equal amounts. Chef Maurice swore by the latter as part of his secret recipe for copper pan cleaner.

The lack of traffic meant they were now directly behind their prey, who seemed oblivious, bopping along in their car to whichever hair-gel-endorsing young male was dominating the pop charts that week.

"Where do you reckon they're going?"

"I do not know, but I am hoping there is food."

A few minutes later, they followed the VW Beetle into the car park of an old pub building of similar construction to Le Cochon Rouge, but in much worse repair. To add insult to injury, this particular pub had been converted into a bar-cum-nightclub, its name picked out in fluorescent tubing.

"'The Office'," read Arthur, as they pulled up on the other side of the car park. "Presumably named so that you're technically telling the truth when you phone home saying you're stuck here at midnight with your secretary."

"You have a secretary?"

"Only Horace. And he's not so good at the filing."

They watched the two girls complete their requisite reapplication of make-up, then shimmy out of their car and into The Office.

Inside, the owners had decided upon a monochrome theme, with dingy black carpet, black walls and black painted booths. Even the barman's teeth were black.

However, the decor—or lack thereof—didn't seem to be deterring the local crowd, mostly made up of trendy-looking youths in their late teens and early twenties, decked out in outfits that seemed to consist of a strategic combination of rips and tears, and boasting enough piercings to set off airport security with a single earlobe.

Just by stepping through the door, Arthur and Chef Maurice probably doubled the average age in the room.

They stopped at the bar to pick up a pint of locally brewed ale for Arthur and a large brandy and bag of pork scratchings for Chef Maurice, then wandered with studied nonchalance over to a booth by the far wall, which sat back-to-back with a larger booth containing the two girls they'd just tailed, along with an assortment of jaded youths of both sexes, their faces mostly obscured in the low lighting.

" . . . didn't come out on Monday?"

"None of your business what I get up to in my free time."

"Bet PJ's mum didn't let him out to play, that's why."

"Don't talk to me about my mum," sniped the voice named PJ. "You won't believe the rubbish she's been having me do this holiday."

"Like cleaning your room, I'll bet . . . "

On the other side of the booth, one of the girls was recounting her day.

" . . . so then we got up and drove over to Beakley, tried going round to Ollie's, but—"

"You did *what*?" That was PJ again, who had the kind of high-pitched whiny voice that makes one itch to apply some boot to the speaker's behind.

"Went over to Ollie's. Don't worry, we parked up the hill like usual, no one saw us."

"Jeez," added the other girl, "you get so wound up about your mate—"

"He's not my mate, and—"

"—and anyway, he wasn't even in."

"Of course he wasn't in, don't you read the papers? He got murdered up in Farnley Woods last week!"

Far from producing the hushed awe that this news possibly deserved, the two girls leapt upon this tidbit like birds on the early worm.

"You're freaking kidding me—"

"How, where, what, you've gotta tell me—"

"I never liked the way he looked at me—"

"Have they found the murderer yet?"

Another male voice roused itself from its pint to relay the tale of the forager's sad demise, roughly as it had been recounted every day since in the local paper—which had been bolstering their coverage with snippets from concerned neighbours (Mrs Eldridge), local residents (Mrs Eldridge) and the village leaders (Mrs Eldridge).

"That's crazy," breathed one of the girls. "Do you think the police will find out about—"

Several voices shushed her into silence.

"Did anyone see you today?" said the voice of PJ. "Because if they did—"

"No one saw us," said one of the girls. "And even if they did, we weren't doing anything wrong." She gasped, then giggled. "Wait, you didn't do it, did you?"

"Don't be daft," said PJ sharply.

"You did say you owed him—"

"I paid him off ages ago. More's the pity," the youth muttered.

"So the papers haven't said anything about Ollie and all the—"

"Shhhhh! Honestly, Chrissy . . . "

The conversation continued in lowered tones. Arthur and Chef Maurice paused, drinks halfway to their lips, and sat up higher in their seats to listen.

After a bit, Arthur was forced to remove the bag of loud crunchy pork scratchings from Chef Maurice's reach.

Then they listened some more.

Patrick cleared his throat, adjusted his glasses, and took one final look at the bouquet in his hand—were carnations good or bad? He'd been too embarrassed to ask Mrs Jenkins, who ran the Beakley post office, which also served as the local flower shop, newsagents and tobacconist—and knocked on the front door of PC Lucy's cottage.

An elderly man, wearing an embroidered waistcoat and red velvet trousers, opened the door.

They stared at each other.

"I'm, uh . . . does Lucy live here?"

"Ah, yes." The old man looked a trifle disappointed. "I did think I was getting on a bit to be receiving young men with flowery bouquets," he said, adding a rather disconcerting wink. "You'll find your young lady upstairs in Flat B." He gestured to the narrow staircase behind him.

"Oh," said Patrick. "You're her landlord, then?"

"Ha, I wish. I'm only renting too, just the bottom flat. Flat A, that's me."

Patrick looked around the hallway, which was filled with old books, jazzy paintings and a long sideboard carved with elephants.

"This is Flat A?"

"That's right."

"So . . . Flat B is inside Flat A?"

The old man stroked his goatee.

"Never thought of it like that, but I suppose you're right. Still, we rub along just fine, the two of us. Wasn't too sure at first, her working for The Authority and all, but she's a nice gel, ever so polite. Knows a closed door's a closed door, if you know what I mean."

Another wink was deployed in Patrick's direction.

"And what's this? Pink carnations, for a lady? We can't be having that . . . "

He plucked the bunch out of Patrick's hands and disappeared into his back room. Patrick stood there, frozen, unsure what the protocol was in such cases of blatant horticultural theft.

"Um," he said, to the world in general.

The old man returned a moment later, holding a beautiful white rose.

"Had a dozen delivered just the other day. Never know when you'll be needing one," he added cryptically. He pressed the stem into Patrick's hand.

"Thanks, um, Mr . . . "

"Karl."

"Thanks, Karl."

"That's Mister Karl, to you," said the old man sharply.

"Um, sorry, Mister Karl."

The old man nodded. "Right, up you go, sonny. And don't be coming back down these stairs too soon." With that, he disappeared into his living room and shut the door, before Patrick could reply.

He noticed, though, that Mister Karl's door hadn't quite closed fully.

He climbed the stairs, ducking to avoid a low beam that, judging by the dents in it, had already disqualified a number of previous suitors, and knocked on the door of Flat B.

Light spilled out and down the stairs as the door was flung back. PC Lucy leaned in the doorway, one hand climbing the door frame, a wooden spoon in the other.

"Why, hello there," she said. Her hair was dishevelled, falling around her face in messy waves. "I've just finished cooking. Come on in."

Patrick sniffed. There was an odd smell drifting about in the kitchen. Something that reminded him of—

"Oooo, you brought me flowers?"

"Well, flower."

PC Lucy threw the spoon in the sink, then plucked up the rose and took a deep sniff. "My favourite." Her nose wrinkled. "I think. It's gorgeous, anyway."

She put the rose down and walked, somewhat unsteadily, over to the front door.

"As are you," she added, closing the door with a meaningful click.

"Um ..." Patrick glanced around as she sashayed towards him. There was a wine bottle on the table, cork out, but it looked full. "Are you sure you're feeling—"

It was at this point that PC Lucy kissed him.

It would have been a rather wonderful moment, aside from the momentary confusion of having an attractive

149

woman launch herself at him, lips first, for no apparent reason. She had her hands in his hair, her skin smelt of lavender soap, and her body was pushed up against his own in a manner that suggested that being just good friends wasn't necessarily at the forefront of her mind.

It would have all been rather wonderful, if she hadn't at that point pulled back with a sudden look of panic, run over to the kitchen sink, and started throwing up.

CHAPTER 15

Chef Maurice hammered on the cottage's front door, with Arthur lurking reluctantly behind.

"Maurice, don't you think this can wait—"

The door swung open, to reveal the distinguished countenance of Mister Karl.

"Why, Mister Maurice, what a pleasure! Do come in. And Arthur too!" Mister Karl held the door open and ushered them into the hallway.

"*Bonsoir*, Monsieur Karl. It is good to see you too." Chef Maurice bowed slightly.

It had always puzzled Arthur how, despite their completely divergent interests, Chef Maurice and Mister Karl seemed to get along just fine. Perhaps it was because they both loved to talk and rarely listened to what the other person was saying. Plus Mister Karl was known to keep quite a good collection of vintage port.

"Can I get you gentlemen something to drink? I've just opened a rather good '77 . . . "

"Ah, I am afraid we are here to visit Mademoiselle Lucy."

"Lucy? My, my, she's a popular one tonight. She's already had one gentleman caller. Your sous-chef, in fact."

"He is still here?"

"I think I can say, most undoubtedly."

"Well, let's not disturb them, then," said Arthur, turning to go.

"*Non, non*, this is too important. We must let Mademoiselle Lucy know at once what we have discovered!"

He started up the stairs but was pulled back by Arthur.

Mister Karl coughed discreetly. "I don't think that this would be a particularly good time to disturb them."

Chef Maurice pulled a battered wristwatch out of his jacket. "It is only nine o'clock. They must surely still be eating dinner," he said, in the tone of a man for whom mealtimes were sacrosanct.

"You'd think so," said Mister Karl drily, "but I think you'll find young people these days are rather more impatient than our generation."

"But it is imperative that we—"

"Ahem." Mister Karl coughed again, and gestured towards his back room. "Perhaps you should . . . judge for yourselves . . ."

Through the door they found a tiny kitchen, a small but well-perfumed bathroom and Mister Karl's bedroom, which involved far too much purple silk and tasselled pillows for Arthur's liking.

"Our flats have the same layout, you see. So that's Lucy's bedroom, right above mine. Makes me blush, it does. I never realised how thin these floors are," said Mister Karl, displaying no such evidence of embarrassment.

From above, though faint through the floorboards, was the unmistakable rumble of Patrick's voice, and a female voice presumably belonging to PC Lucy. It was moaning.

If he hadn't known better, Arthur would have said it sounded like someone experiencing severe gastrointestinal pains. As it was, Arthur felt himself go bright red.

"I think we better go back outside. Quickly."

They reconvened in Mister Karl's opulently decorated front room to ponder their options. In the end, Chef Maurice compromised on writing a long-winded note detailing the results of their stake-out, complete with many underlinings and exclamation marks.

They agreed they would knock politely on PC Lucy's flat and, pending no answer, would slip the note under the door and not return until at least seven o'clock the next morning.

In the meantime, Chef Maurice was not to climb any nearby trees, throw stones at any windows, nor set fire to Mister Karl's flat in an effort to gain PC Lucy's attentions.

Terms and conditions thus agreed upon, they trooped up the stairs in single file to deliver their missive.

Arthur knocked gently on the door.

"There you go," he said, when no one answered. "They're busy, now let's go and—"

"Bah, that is not how you knock on a door!"

Chef Maurice manoeuvred his bulk around Arthur and raised a fist, but before he could knock, the door swung

153

open to reveal Patrick, looking dishevelled in only a T-shirt and boxers.

"Thank goodness you're here!" he said.

Arthur and Mister Karl exchanged a puzzled look.

"Lucy's really sick. I've phoned the doctor, but he said he won't get here for another few hours . . . " He looked at them wildly, running his hands through his hair. "I think it might be something she ate before I got here. I think it was some kind of mushroom . . . "

They all stood in PC Lucy's kitchen.

"It's a bit early for reindeers," said Arthur, for lack of anything else to say.

Patrick looked down at his boxers. "Oh. Well, I didn't expect anyone to see them . . . "

"God favours the prepared," said Mister Karl.

"I had to take off my jeans and shirt after Lucy threw up all over them. She did try not to," he added, always the gentleman.

Chef Maurice wandered over to the kitchen table, which was still set for two, with pristine white plates and empty glasses. He picked up the wine bottle and his eyes went wide.

"Patrick, you must marry this *femme*. At once!" He poured himself a glass and drew a deep sniff. "Ahhh, Gevrey-Chambertin, '79. Domaine des Moines. Like an old friend . . . "

"Maurice, I really don't think you should be drinking that."

154

"But wine, it is made to be drunk."

"Yes, but not when it belongs to someone else . . . "

There was another moan from the direction of the bedroom.

"I better get back to Lucy," said Patrick, grabbing a roll of kitchen paper.

The others followed him, Chef Maurice with a glass in one hand and a buttered wedge of soft seeded bread in the other. It had been a long time since those pork scratchings.

PC Lucy was lying on her bed, fully clothed, her face covered by her pillow.

"I just want to curl up and die," she groaned. A bucket, as yet unused, sat next to the bed.

It had been a while since Chef Maurice had jousted in the lists of love, but unless things had changed dramatically in the time intervening, this was not how an amorous evening was meant to go.

"What has happened?"

Patrick rubbed his eyes. "I don't know. I turned up for dinner, she let me in, then suddenly she started throwing up."

"Just like that? She did not do anything, eat anything, just before that?"

Patrick's ears reddened. "Well . . . "

The pillow lowered, and one blue eye, rather unfocused, peered out into the room. It took in the bulk of Chef Maurice, seated at the foot of the bed, Patrick, who was

155

standing nearby, Arthur in the doorway, and Mister Karl, who was busy rearranging the closet by season and colour.

"How many of you are there in here?" croaked PC Lucy.

Chef Maurice looked around. "There is just me, Arthur, Patrick and Monsieur Karl."

"And the flamingos and the maroon elephant . . . ?" Her head slumped back and she put a hand across her eyes. "Someone stop the ceiling from waving like that, please . . . "

Chef Maurice looked over to Arthur, who nodded. They headed for the kitchen and the large pot of risotto, which was now a sludgy grey mass with burnt bits at the bottom.

Strange aromas emanated from the pot.

"I am not an expert in these matters," said Chef Maurice, sniffing the spoon, "but I think these are not dried cèpes. But why would Mademoiselle Lucy . . . ?"

Their gaze fell on the open plastic box in the corner.

There was another groan from the bedroom.

"Did I just hallucinate a Chef Maurice?" said PC Lucy's voice.

Chef Maurice hurried back to the room.

"*Non, mademoiselle*, I assure you I am quite real."

PC Lucy pulled her pillow back over her face. Chef Maurice didn't quite catch what she muttered, but Patrick looked rather scandalised.

"Mademoiselle Lucy, you must listen. We have important reconnaissance regarding the murder of Monsieur Ollie. Do you hear me?"

"Mmmph . . . "

"We happened upon a public house in Cowton—"

"Since when do you go drinking in Cowton?" said Patrick suspiciously.

"—and we were present to overhear a discussion about Monsieur Ollie, and his trade in the most illegal of—"

"Magic mushrooms," groaned PC Lucy, coming up for air. "Damn magic mushrooms. I recognise the smell now. Can someone pass that bucket—"

They all left the room to give PC Lucy some private time with the bucket and the maroon elephants.

"So *that's* why it smelt so weird in here," said Patrick, poking at the risotto. "I thought it was her cooking."

"I heard that . . . " came a weak voice from the other room.

"Don't worry," said Arthur. "Chances are, she'll have forgotten this whole evening by tomorrow."

"In that case," said Chef Maurice, rummaging in the cupboards for two more wine glasses, "we must make sure this fine bottle does not go to waste . . . "

CHAPTER 16

The next morning, Arthur and Chef Maurice took a drive over to Gloucestershire, a paper bag full of mushrooms carefully balanced on Chef Maurice's knee.

Miss Fey opened the door as they pulled up in front of her cottage.

"Good morning, gentlemen. Do come in. I have to say, I was quite intrigued when you called me. I've just put the kettle on. Can I tempt you with a cup of tea?"

Arthur and Chef Maurice agreed that they could indeed be tempted.

"Is it me, or is there something different about her today?" said Arthur to Chef Maurice, as they settled themselves into the same chintz armchairs.

Chef Maurice, whose sometimes keen observational powers did not extend to sartorial matters, shrugged.

The hair, that had definitely changed, thought Arthur. Gone was the messy plait, replaced by a neat and complicated bun arrangement that probably took four mirrors and step-by-step diagrams to assemble. The flowery dress had been cast aside in favour of freshly pressed brown trousers, a blue blouse and, oddly enough, a white lab coat.

Miss Fey caught Arthur staring and gave him a small knowing smile.

"I'll bet you're thinking, what happened to that crotchety old biddy we met the other day?"

"Well . . . "

"She's just a figment of the imagination, I'm afraid, though I'd appreciate it if you'd go ahead and write about her all the same." She sighed. "I'm afraid that when it comes to our countryside, the reading public still favour the idea of the nice little old lady, poking about the hedgerows and mossy banks. Foraging is all the rage currently, while sadly the serious study of mycology is a closed book to most."

"Mike who?" asked Chef Maurice, as he sipped his tea and pulled the Victoria sponge cake a little closer.

"Mycology," said Arthur. "The study of mushrooms and other fungi."

"Very good," said Miss Fey. "It's a truly fascinating subject. Do you know in this country we've been using mushrooms for centuries, not just as a foodstuff, but for medicinal properties, for kindling fires, even as part of religious rituals?"

"Medicinal? Really?"

"Oh yes, many mushrooms are well known for their antibacterial and antiviral properties, as well as other health benefits. In fact, my lab is close to patenting a cholesterol-lowering serum based on the enoki mushroom."

"Your lab?" said Arthur, struggling to keep up.

"We're part of the Oxford Department of Plant Pathology, but they don't like to talk about us much. I'm afraid mycological funding is terribly hard to come by. You could say my little mushroom-selling business is a key part of the lab."

"Keeps you in the test tubes, eh?"

"Something like that, yes." Miss Fey manoeuvred a lump of sugar into her tea. "Now tell me about this mushroom your friend ingested yesterday."

Chef Maurice handed over the paper bag. PC Lucy had kept back most of the sample to send over to the county forensics lab, but it could be weeks before they got an answer, she'd said. So in the meantime, she'd reluctantly allowed Chef Maurice and Arthur to take away a few specimens to show their 'mushroom expert'.

Miss Fey peered into the bag and sniffed. "Yes, definitely one of the *psilocybe* family, though it's hard to say much more when they're cut and dried like this. Psychedelic mushrooms, we used to call them back in my day. You don't have any fresh specimens, do you?"

Arthur started to shake his head, but Chef Maurice coughed and produced a smaller paper bag from his jacket.

"I found these in an unsorted bag of mushrooms I took from Monsieur Ollie's fridge." He tipped a handful of black spindly mushrooms into his hand.

"You broke into his cottage *again*?"

Chef Maurice looked hurt. "I do not break in anywhere. And these are from the first time, when I was attacked, you remember?"

Arthur gave up. Chef Maurice had been known to sneak entire layered cheesecakes out of the walk-in fridge without anyone noticing. A bag of mushrooms was probably child's play.

Miss Fey was inspecting the underside of one sample.

"Hmmm, yes, the gill structure seems right . . . Interesting . . . " She looked up at them. "I'll need to take this out back to the lab. You're welcome to follow."

"Certainly," said Arthur, collecting up his hat. "It'd be fascinating, I'm sure. Come on, Maurice."

"You can bring the Victoria sponge cake too, as long as you stay away from my petri dishes," said Miss Fey to Chef Maurice.

Miss Fey, thought Arthur, was turning out to be a pretty good judge of character.

At the end of the garden, Miss Fey's shed-turned-mycology-lab bore more resemblance to Ollie's ransacked kitchen than to a cutting-edge hub of scientific endeavour.

There were mushrooms everywhere. Fresh, dried, dissected, soaking in solution, arranged in labelled jars. The walls were covered in painstakingly drawn diagrams of mushroom cross-sections.

"What is this?" said Chef Maurice, prodding a giant black clam-shaped specimen, the size of a roast turkey.

"That's a hoof fungus, also known as the tinder polypore. Completely inedible, I'm afraid, but very good for starting fires."

"And this one?" Chef Maurice pointed to a fleshy grey-brown mushroom.

"That's a birch bracket. It has some interesting anti-inflammatory properties as well as—" She stopped, as she saw Chef Maurice's eyes glaze over. "It's terribly bitter, you wouldn't want to cook with it."

"Ah, *très bien*."

"I'm glad you gentlemen brought your coats, it gets a little nippy in here," said Miss Fey, pulling a thick woollen scarf off a hook on the shed door, the colour combination of which was of such a level of hideousness it could only have been knitted by a much-cherished relative. "Now if you'll just excuse me a few moments . . . "

Thus followed several minutes of cutting, mixing, pipetting and staring down a large microscope.

Arthur heard Chef Maurice gasp. His friend was pointing with an urgent finger at the door, where, hanging from the same hook, was a black woollen balaclava.

Arthur spread his hands and shrugged. People were allowed to own balaclavas, especially if they spent their time roaming around the damp woods.

Chef Maurice waved his own hands, contriving to suggest, via the medium of mime, that they should tie up Miss Fey and conduct a thorough search of the premises for Hamilton right away.

162

Arthur twiddled his finger in the international hand gesture for 'you're a raving loony'.

"As I suspected," said Miss Fey, still staring into her microscope and oblivious to the pantomime going on behind her, "this is an example of the *psilocybe morticis*, one of the strongest hallucinogens in the *psilocybe* family. You said that your friend suffered some ill effects after consuming the dried variety?"

"She was sick as a bitch," said Chef Maurice.

Miss Fey gave him a disapproving look.

"Dog, Maurice," whispered Arthur. "You mean 'sick as a dog'."

"But Mademoiselle Lucy is female."

"The phrase does not alter."

"Ah."

"This particular species is rare in Britain and, unfortunately, quite valuable to a . . . certain section of the population. Such a shame that some people misuse the mushroom family for such purposes."

"How valuable, would you say?" asked Arthur.

Miss Fey tilted her head. "Why do you ask?"

"Well, imagine that these mushrooms might have come from Ollie Meadows' house. Not to be overly dramatic, but are they valuable enough that someone might have put Ollie out of business—permanently—to get hold of his supply?"

Miss Fey gave a little shrug. "It's possible." She fixed Arthur with her level stare. "Some people will do just about anything for money."

Hamilton buried his nose in his makeshift bed, which seemed to consist of a pile of old T-shirts.

He'd not been badly treated, it was true. The sow nuts kept coming, along with the occasional treat of cut-up pieces of carrot.

Even so, being kept in a crate in a room that smelt strongly of humans, or at least one particular human, did not fit well with what he viewed as his higher purpose.

Plus, life in a crate was all extremely boring. He'd been quite taken with his recent adventures; the fat man with the abundant sow nuts, the truffle-hunting endeavours, and the big field, all to himself. And before that, life with his previous owners hadn't been too bad either (before that dark day in the woods, of course). They'd been a pleasant enough, if unexciting, family, giving him the run of the small garden, buying him a squeaky ball, and feeding him the odd tidbits off their plentiful dinner table. It was from them that he'd first had a taste of heavenly truffle.

There was the creak of footsteps outside the room and the sound of raised voices.

"—meant to *do* with it?"

"I told you before, just put the creature out of its misery."

"Unlike some people I know, I don't think killing things is always the answer!"

There was a sharp intake of breath. "I've told you not to talk about that . . . that incident. If it hadn't been for you and your big mouth, Meadows would never have started poking around up here in the first place."

"Aren't you worried that they'll trace the shotgun—"

"No, I'm not! As long as you don't get any big ideas about letting that pig out of here. You keep it, or get rid of it *properly*."

Hamilton wasn't too sure what was going on—it was all Human to him—but he was pretty certain he didn't like the tone of the voices, especially that of the second speaker.

He'd waited long enough now for his new owner to come and rescue him. It was time to take things into his own trotters and start planning an escape.

Else, it sounded like he was heading for the terminal Pig Sleep.

Driving back into Beakley, they were hailed down by Mrs Eldridge, who was crouched behind the hedge in her front garden, waving a handkerchief that had seen better days.

Arthur pulled over onto the grassy verge and they got out.

"Is everything all right?"

"Shhhh!" She grabbed them each by an elbow and pulled them down into the shrubbery. "You need to call the police, right now!"

"Why, what's happened?"

"There's a strange man in Ollie's cottage. I saw him sneak round the back just now. If I hadn't just been passing by the window . . . "

165

"It is the same man you saw before, *madame*?"

"That's right, the one who was skulking around here the other day. Now he's robbing a dead man's cottage. Some people have no respect. Just look at him, wandering around like he owns the place."

Three pairs of eyes peered over the window ledge into the front room.

Sure enough, a tall, thick-set man with a dark beard was strolling around the living room, riffling through papers and looking in the desk drawers. He seemed fairly relaxed, as far as burglars went.

"Is it normal for them to smoke a pipe when on a job?" said Arthur. The man had now exited the room, presumably to continue his leisurely perusal upstairs. "He doesn't seem to be stealing anything."

"Still, we must call Mademoiselle Lucy at once! This could be the man that pignapped *le pauvre* Hamilton."

"Now wait, Maurice, no need to go jumping to—"

There was a click behind them.

"Hands up where I can see them," growled a voice from behind. Arthur turned around and stood up, banging his head on the window ledge, and found himself staring down the barrel of a shotgun.

CHAPTER 17

Patrick stood at the stove, listlessly stirring a pan of pomme purée.

"Cheer up, luv," said Dorothy, who was busying herself at the sink, trimming a bunch of wild flowers for the little vases in the dining room. "It's only been a few hours. She'll be calling you back by the end of the day, I'm sure of it."

Patrick was less sure. He'd heard that women could get a bit funny about you seeing them without their make-up on, or in sports clothes, or under whatever criteria they deemed as looking less than their best.

Helping them hold their hair back as they projectile vomited into a bucket probably counted somewhere in that category.

"Did you at least get in a kiss?"

"Well. Sort of . . . "

"There's no 'sort of' in these matters, luv."

"She was a bit, well, intoxicated."

"Patrick Merland! I would have thought better of you than that, taking advantage of a lady—"

"I didn't! She's the one who started it."

And finished it rather abruptly too, he thought.

He could hear Alf sniggering from somewhere behind a mountain of potatoes.

"Well," said Dorothy, considering this new information, "that's probably all right, then."

Patrick wasn't so sure about this either. At least he hadn't had the chance to really mess things up, he thought, given the circumstances. The doctor had finally turned up around midnight and announced that PC Lucy seemed to have got rid of most of the mushroom toxins of her own accord, and sent her to bed.

Patrick had tried to get some sleep on the couch, which sagged and creaked torturously every time he moved a muscle. He had eventually given up and resorted to tidying the kitchen, throwing away the offending risotto, rearranging the pots and pans and sharpening the knives.

He'd gone through the fridge too, sorting the contents into three shelves: expiring food, expired food, and food that PC Lucy was presumably keeping for sentimental value, given the far-gone use-by dates.

He didn't dare tell Chef Maurice about the sorry lump of hardened cheddar he'd found in the bottom of the fridge, and made a note to present PC Lucy with a wheel of *brie de meaux* next time he went round.

If there was going to be a next time.

* * *

The barrel of the gun lowered, as if the bearer had realised that any group consisting of Chef Maurice, Arthur and Mrs Eldridge could only pose a threat by pure accident.

"What are you lot doing peering into the windows of my house?" he boomed.

There was the twang of the Midlands in his accent, mixed in with a dash of *pomodori* and *parmigiano*.

"It's not your house," snapped Mrs Eldridge, advancing with her cane. "This house belongs to poor Ollie Meadows, God rest his soul wherever it is. So be off with you and all your sneaking around. Be sure to empty your pockets first, mind."

The man grunted and reached into his jacket. For a moment, Arthur thought he was about to draw a gun, until he realised the man already had one in his hand.

An official-looking letter-headed paper was withdrawn and waved at them. "Ollie is my nephew. The contents of the house pass to my sister, Maria. But she is in Torino, so I have come to collect his belongings."

Mrs Eldridge grabbed the paper and pulled out her reading glasses, while Chef Maurice peered over her shoulder.

"Hmmm, it all seems leg-git," she pronounced after a while. She narrowed her eyes at the newcomer. "Welcome to Beakley, Mr Mannozzi. Don't think I won't be watching you."

With that, she tottered back over to her half of the cottage and slammed the front door. A few moments later, they heard the window upstairs creak open.

"Luciano Mannozzi, pleased to meet you," said the man, proffering a large calloused hand.

"Arthur Wordington-Smythe." He returned the handshake, while Chef Maurice stood there silently, regarding their visitor with arms folded. "Are you planning to stay here long?"

"No, the landlord has given me a few days to clear out the cottage. Then he will rent it out again, he says. Anyway, I must soon go back up to my business."

"Your business?"

"I am an importer of foods from Italy," said Luciano proudly. "Cheese, olive oil, *aceto balsamico*, the special pastas—"

"Do you supply to restaurants or to consumers?" asked Chef Maurice, in tones that indicated there was only one correct answer.

"Restaurants, for the most," said Luciano, looking down at Chef Maurice's steel-capped boots. "And the occasional deli."

"Ah, *très bien*. I have been in need of a good supplier of Italian cheese. The burrata I last received from my current supplier was like a rubber ball—"

There was a bark, and a small, scruffy dog tore round the corner and came to a halt at Luciano's feet.

"Ah, and who is this?"

"This is Tufo," said Luciano.

"Lively-looking fellow," said Arthur.

"*Bonjour, petit chien.*" Chef Maurice bent down and

lifted the dog up to face him. Tufo hung there in his arms, turning his nose questioningly to his master.

"Well behaved, too," said Arthur, thinking about what Horace would do if a stranger tried to pick him up. That said, in Horace's case you'd probably need to hire a forklift truck first.

"Your friend, what is he doing?" asked Luciano, as Chef Maurice raised Tufo's nose to his own and proceeded to sniff loudly.

"He's, um, become quite interested in dogs lately."

"I see," said Luciano, folding his arms.

"A good dog," said Chef Maurice, lowering Tufo to the ground and patting him on the head.

"I'm terribly sorry to hear about your nephew," said Arthur. "He was well-liked in the village." A stretch of the truth perhaps, but perfectly acceptable in these circumstances.

Luciano gave a gruff chuckle. "I doubt it, but it is kind of you to say so. He was always trouble, little Ollie. I told Maria, she should have kept him closer to home. Gets it from his father's side, the English side—he was never well-behaved like a good Italian boy."

"Mmmm," said Arthur, who had encountered more than his fair share of flamboyant, foul-mouthed, pan-flinging Italian chefs in his food critic career thus far. "Did you used to come down to Beakley much?"

"No, not often. I have not been here since last winter, in fact."

"Oh, really? That's odd, because Mrs Eldridge—"

An elbow to his ribs stopped Arthur mid-flow.

"We must go now," said Chef Maurice, shaking Luciano's hand and patting Tufo one last time. "But you will send me a list of your cheeses, yes?"

Arthur hurried after Chef Maurice, rubbing his ribs. "What was all that about? And what were you doing to that poor dog? Don't try to pretend you're suddenly a dog person."

"I am not. And neither is Monsieur Mannozzi. You see, that dog, it is not his."

"What makes you say that?"

"On its breath, I smelt the distinct smell of white truffles. It is a truffle dog! And then I remember this."

He pulled out the Polaroid that Tara had shown them the other day, down at the Helping Paws Pet Sanctuary.

It was slightly blurred, but it was definitely the same dog that they'd just met.

"That dog, *mon ami*, is the missing dog of Monsieur Ollie!"

Down at the Cowton police station, PC Lucy was grappling with a case of social etiquette.

"You have to call him back," said PC Sara, scrolling through some reports on her computer screen. "It'd be rude, otherwise."

"No I don't. I didn't ask him to call. We had a date, it was horrendous, there's no need for me to speak to him ever again."

"Apart from the fact you have the hots for him."

"I do *not* have the hots for him."

"So the fact that you threw yourself across the room at him the minute he walked in the door . . . ?"

"It was the mushrooms talking."

"I doubt there was much talking going on at that point," said PC Sara with a smirk.

"And then I threw up all over him!"

"But he stayed to make sure you were okay. I call that gentlemanly."

"Plus, he tidied up my fridge. What kind of man tidies up a fridge for *fun*?"

"He *is* a chef," said PC Sara, as if pleading first offense.

"And I think he rearranged my wardrobe," PC Lucy added darkly. "Anyway, he's probably just calling to get me to pay for his dry cleaning."

"So call him back and see."

Thankfully, her phone buzzed at this point. Waving PC Sara away, she pressed 'answer'.

"Hello? Gavistone speaking— Oh, hi, Mr Manchot. Yes, I'm feeling much better, thank you for asking. Actually, I had a question, did someone go through my wardrobe last night? Oh, Mister Karl? Well, that's a relief."

From the other side of the desk, PC Sara gave her a big thumbs up.

"Yes, I'm at the station— What? Maurice— I mean, Mr Manchot, do you really think— Okay, I'll go over and have a word tomorrow when— No! Stay right where you

173

are! Under no circumstances should you make a citizen's arrest— No, I don't care what you've read— Okay, okay, I'll be there right away!"

She hung up.

"Maurice seems to think he's caught Ollie's murderer."

"That's good of him."

"And his dog."

"The murderer's dog? Or Ollie's dog? Was the dog the murderer?"

"I'm a bit confused on that point, too."

"Well, there you go, case closed. Now you can phone that poor fellow back and offer to do his laundry. At his place."

PC Lucy shot her a warning look. "I'll be back in a while. Let the chief know, okay?"

"Sure. Don't go arresting anyone you shouldn't."

A vision of Chef Maurice passed through PC Lucy's mind.

"I'll try my best not to."

CHAPTER 18

It was not an arrest, nor was it an interrogation; that much was clear. The police merely wanted to have a little chat with Mr Luciano Mannozzi, to clear up a few matters, and if he'd be so kind as to pop down to the station at a convenient moment, it would be most appreciated. They just happened to have a car waiting right now— Oh, how kind of him, his co-operation would of course be duly noted.

Luciano now sat in Cowton Police Station's only interview room, which was empty apart from a few pieces of furniture; a look that spoke less of menace and more of budgetary constraints. The door was left unlocked. However, two uniformed constables sat outside on either side, discussing the cricket.

PC Lucy had failed to prevent Chef Maurice and Arthur from entering the station itself. However, she'd instructed the two constables to keep them out of the interview room using any means possible.

This suited them fine, as Chef Maurice soon discovered that the interview room backed onto an empty corridor behind the main office, with a conveniently located air vent high up on the wall. Chef Maurice and Arthur settled themselves into a couple of plastic chairs, and Chef Maurice pulled out a pair of tuna-and-caper-filled baguettes from his jacket.

The interview, from what they could gather through the vent, was not going well. Despite his initial co-operative air, Luciano was clearly not too happy about PC Lucy's particular line of questioning.

"Tufo is *my* dog, why do you not listen? I lent him to Ollie—for a sum, which he never paid me—so I come to get Tufo and Ollie gave him back. That is the end of the story."

"So why did Mr Meadows borrow your dog in the first place?"

Silence.

"I understand your business involves the import of Italian foodstuffs into the UK, predominantly from the Piedmont region?"

"Yes, that is correct."

"And these foodstuffs also include the white Alba truffle?"

A pause. "Yes."

"Which, according to your website, you pick yourself in the winter months with the help of your dog? A trained truffle dog?"

"This has nothing to do with my nephew!"

"I'll ask again, Mr Mannozzi. Why did Mr Meadows wish to borrow your truffle dog? Had he, in fact, found an unknown truffle ground in this vicinity and wished to profit from it?"

"Ha! My nephew was always one for schemes, for rumours. Perhaps someone told him stories of truffles in this area. Lies, and more lies. Everyone knows there are no Alba truffles in England."

"But you still went and lent him your dog?"

"Yes, he is family, it is expected."

"Plus, he offered you a substantial sum of money, didn't he?"

There was the sound of Luciano shifting uncomfortably in his chair. "To train a good truffle dog is a long process. They are valuable animals. He was lucky I was willing to make him the loan."

"And how much did he offer to pay you to borrow your dog?"

Another scrape of chair against concrete floor.

"Two thousand pounds."

They heard PC Lucy whistle. "That's a lot of money for borrowing a dog."

"Which he did not pay me," growled Luciano.

"So at that point, you came and took back your dog?"

"Yes."

"And when was this?"

"On the Sunday last."

"That's interesting. Because you told one of his neighbours today that you hadn't been to Beakley in several months."

"It was none of their business."

"I see. So, in fact, you had been here in Beakley last week. The week Ollie went missing."

"Yes, but I did not see him!" Luciano now sounded worried.

"I thought you said that Ollie gave your dog back to you?"

There was a long silence. Then a fist banged on the table.

"Okay! It is like this. I phone my nephew, he tells me some story about Tufo running away from him. This is rubbish, Tufo would never do something like this, he is a good dog. So I come down, no one is at home. So I think to myself that maybe there is a chance my nephew is telling the truth. I go to the animal home, and there is Tufo. He had been lost in the woods, they said. So I take him and go home. That is the end!"

"Did you leave Mr Meadows a note when you visited his cottage? Perhaps one like this?" There was a rustle of paper, then PC Lucy read out: "'Have come to collect my loan, don't give me any more lies if you know what's good for you.' A threat, Mr Mannozzi?"

"I did not mean it! Why would I harm my own nephew?"

"He owed you quite a sum of money."

Silence.

"So you came down to Beakley last Sunday, and left this note?"

"Yes, that is what I said."

"So you hadn't been down in Beakley before this?"

Another pause. "No."

Next to Arthur, Chef Maurice threw down his baguette and climbed onto his chair, so his face was level with the vent.

"He lies!" he shouted through the grille. "He was here on the Friday too, Madame Eldridge observed him! And that day, someone broke into Monsieur Ollie's cottage. The first time!"

There was the click of a door, a clatter of footsteps, and PC Lucy appeared round the corner, her cheeks flushed.

"Mr Manchot! Mr Wordington-Smythe! This is a police station, not a picnic ground!" She waved at the half-eaten baguette wrapped in a napkin.

"But it all makes sense!" argued Chef Maurice. "He comes to collect his dog, he follows them up in the woods, but Monsieur Ollie refuses to give him back. Then, in anger, bang! We know he has a gun, he threatened us today with it. So he shoots poor Monsieur Ollie, then he goes home."

"Rubbish!" shouted a distant voice through the grille. "Yes, I come here on the Friday too, I wait for Ollie all day, but he does not come home. So I leave a note. Ollie is my own blood, my sister's child. I would never do anything to—"

"And you stole his map too! So you could find the truffles that Monsieur Ollie found!"

"Map? What map? Hah, my nephew knows nothing of truffles, how could he find a patch, even with Tufo's help?"

"So you deny it?"

"Of course I deny it, I have done nothing!"

"You broke into Monsieur Ollie's cottage on the Friday, *non*?"

"Yes, but only to find Tufo! He was not there, so I go!"

"And you also deny that you steal my pig? And then send me bacon?"

PC Lucy looked at Arthur. "What's he on about now?"

"I'll tell you later."

Luciano was now yelling at the top of his voice. "Pig?! Why would I want a pig?"

"Hamilton is a truffle pig!"

"Hah, truffle pigs, they are useless! They will bite your arm off, just to steal the truffle! You can keep your stupid truffle pig."

"You will not talk about my Hamilton in such a way!"

"Enough of this!"

They heard stomping footsteps and the sound of a metal door being flung against the wall.

One of the constables put his head around the corner. "Uh, PC Gavistone . . . "

"Let him go," said PC Lucy irritably. "There's no reason for us to keep him here."

"Bah!" said Chef Maurice. He turned to PC Lucy. "If you do not find my little Hamilton soon, I will . . . "

He trailed off, searching for a suitable punishment.

180

"I will forbid my sous-chef from ever setting foot in your home again!"

After Chef Maurice and Arthur had taken their leave, along with the remains of their picnic, PC Lucy sagged down into a chair.

She wondered if Chef Maurice would make good on his threat.

It would, she thought, at least solve the problem of having to call Patrick back.

It was a gloomy little group that sat round the table in the kitchens of Le Cochon Rouge, quiet in the post-lunchtime lull. Rain dripped down outside and the kettle steamed up the window panes.

Chef Maurice was hunched over the table, staring morosely at a spare copy of the Missing Hamilton flyer. So far, only two people had called, both to ask where they could purchase their own micro-pigs.

Patrick was alternately watching the phone and making his way through a book entitled: *What Women Think (But Don't Want To Think They Think)*.

Arthur was dealing with the aftermath of his latest review, of a restaurant in London's trendy Shoreditch district that only served fried chicken cutlets and scrambled eggs. ("Which to order first, the chicken or the egg? After sampling both, the cutlet burnt on one side, perilously raw on the other, the eggs having reached a peculiar rubberised texture that reminds one of a slice of Pirelli's finest, the answer is an emphatic 'neither'.") The review had apparently angered the young-chef-cum-farmer-cum-restaurateur and had resulted in an envelope of chicken droppings being delivered with the morning post.

Every household has one person who dutifully slices open the mail, and another person who hides unopened mail under piles of newspapers and lets letters get lost behind the hallway table, and in the Wordington-Smythe household, the designated letter-opener was Meryl. Hence why Arthur was now in the serious doghouse and was hiding out at Le Cochon Rouge until his wife's anger cooled down to a gentle simmer.

Only Alf, having spotted a supply gap in the local mushroom market, seemed fairly contented, leafing through a copy of *The Beginner's Guide to Field Foraging*.

So far, he'd reached Chapter 1: Mushrooms, Fun(gus) Friend or Deadly Foe?

"Did you know," he said to the captive audience around the table, "that just one Death Cap mushroom can kill several people, by attacking the liver and kidney cells, with no known antidote?"

"*Très intéressant.*"

"I mean, at least they were dry. And the kitchen table wipes down easily enough. I don't know why she's making such a fuss . . . Women!"

"'Women claim to admire a man of strong intent and mind, who is capable of expressing his opinions in a calm and rational manner.'"

182

Chef Maurice flipped over the flyer and started scribbling. "I must make an arrangement of my thoughts," he muttered to himself. "The rescue of Hamilton is without doubt tied to the solving of the murder of Monsieur Ollie. So I must think.

"First, we have the break-in to Monsieur Ollie's cottage. The first time, on the Friday, Monsieur Mannozzi admits to. According to Monsieur Ollie, nothing was taken. Did he lie? Perhaps something was put there instead? Or is Monsieur Mannozzi telling the truth, he was only looking for Tufo?

"The second time, an old map is stolen. A map of Farnley Woods, made many decades ago. But we have seen this map, it shows nothing of interest. Did Monsieur Ollie add to the map? Mrs Eldridge said that he drew on it. But who would know to take it?"

The rain continued to drum on the windows.

"'Unfortunately, the Death Cap mushroom can easily be confused with the Tawny Grisette, a harmless edible example of the Amanita family, with a delicate flavour best enjoyed on its own or in omelettes.'"

"Then we have the pignapping of Hamilton. To send a warning, it is clear. But a warning of what? Monsieur Ollie searched for truffles. We search for truffles. Who else might search for them?"

"'However, when faced with an angry or upset woman, it is best to avoid calm and rational opinions altogether. Instead, endeavour to see things from her, and only her, point of view. Under no circumstances should you offer up what you view as reasonable solutions to the problem at hand. Especially when expressly asked to do so.'"

"Finally, we have the case of the magic mushrooms. Monsieur Ollie was without doubt part of this illegal trade. There is money in this trade, according to Madame Fey. Did someone owe Monsieur Ollie money? And if so, did they murder him in order to cancel their debt?"

"It's not my fault Horace got his paws all up on the table and they went all over the place . . . "

Chef Maurice slapped his hand down on the flyer. "We need to know more! And we must find those who will tell us. Had Monsieur Ollie truly found truffles in Farnley Woods? Then who did he sell to? Who would know? He seems to have no friends . . . "

"'Women often think they have left you subtle hints about things they like. Unfortunately, these hints are generally only discernible to other women.'" Patrick looked up from his book. "Do you think she didn't like the rose I gave her?"

"Roses! A capital idea. Meryl has a thing for the pink ones . . . "

"*Les fleurs . . . les fleurs sauvages . . .*" muttered Chef Maurice. "Why do I think of flowers?"

"What's that about savage flowers, old chap?"

"Wild flowers, *mon ami*. I am thinking of wild flowers . . ."

Ollie hadn't had many close acquaintances in Beakley. But what was that Miss Fey had said? Something about his many lady friends. Maybe one of them might know something about his shady dealings.

And then he remembered a pot of wild flowers . . .

The afternoon rain clouds were just clearing as Chef Maurice and Arthur swung up the driveway to Laithwaites Manor.

It was time to return to the scene of the crime, thought Chef Maurice, and do some detectoring of his own. Clearly the local police had their minds on other priorities, such as letting hardened pig-stealing criminals shout at him and wander out of their station, and letting their female officers get high on illicit substances and proposition his sous-chef. No, if this crime was to be solved, it would not be solved by the police.

Soon, they were ensconced in Brenda's warm kitchen, with a pot of coffee brewing on the stove and compliments flowing about the frangipane plum tart he'd brought along.

"I just don't know how you get the pastry so nice and even," said Brenda, cutting a generous slice each for her guests and a smaller one for herself.

"It does take much practice," said Chef Maurice, who'd spent the last few months standing over Alf's shoulder as the commis chef rolled out the pastry to just the right depth.

He looked around the tidy kitchen. "You have recovered, *madame*, from the terrible ordeal that happened here just the other day?"

"Indeed I have," said Brenda staunchly. "It makes me mad to think of it now. The nerve of it, kidnapping that defenceless little pig. He put up a good fight, I'll hope you'll know that, Mr Maurice."

There was the disjointed patter of someone coming down the stairs at breakneck speed, then a young man with tousled hair swung his head into the kitchen. He wore woefully tight jeans and a black T-shirt emblazoned with some heavy metal band logo.

"Oh, hi, darling," said Brenda. "Nice to see you finally up. This is Mr Manchot and Mr Wordington-Smythe—you know, the food critic from the England Observer—from over in Beakley. Gentlemen, this is my son, Peter."

The young man grunted as he inspected the fridge's contents.

Brenda gave her guests a maternal 'what can you do?' smile.

"They're all like that, I'm afraid. Don't even see them before midday, and then they just shuffle about until it's dark."

"I was wondering, *madame*, if we might ask you again to describe the intruder who took Hamilton."

"Oh!" Brenda threw a glance at her son, but he seemed oblivious to the conversation. "Well, he was tall, very tall in fact, and broad. Hulking, even."

"And the balaclava he wore, you said it was black. Do you remember what it was made of?"

"Oh my, I'm afraid I don't, it was all such a blur . . . "

186

"Completely understandable," said Arthur. "These things happen so fast."

"Hmph," said Chef Maurice. He was less than impressed with Brenda's abilities of recall, even if she did keep her kitchen in good order. "Do you remember what type of gun he had?"

"A small one, I think . . . yes, small, like the ones in those American TV shows."

"Not a shotgun, then?"

"No, definitely not." She looked at them. "That poacher, he was shot with a shotgun, wasn't he? Do you think it was the same man who—"

"*Non, non, madame*, do not distress yourself. We simply seek more information to help with the search for Hamilton. May we take a walk around the house outside?"

"Of course, please, take your time." Brenda reached down and plopped Missy onto her lap. "Such horrible business," she said, stroking the poodle's curls.

Chef Maurice and Arthur spent a while combing the gravel yard round the side of the house by the kitchens, until Arthur's back decided it had had enough of that particular pursuit.

As they walked, or limped, back to the car, Chef Maurice spotted something wedged into the drain near the front corner of the house. He bent down and used a stick to hook it up.

It was a little pink bobble hat, now sodden with rain and mud.

"A clue?" said Arthur hopefully.

Chef Maurice shook his head. The hat had clearly been dropped at the time of the pignapping, and had been shunted along the gutter by rain over the last few days. As it was, it was simply a soggy reminder of their failure, thus far, in the rescue of poor Hamilton.

He folded the little hat into his handkerchief, and they walked on in silence.

The fine dining restaurant community in Oxfordshire was not a large one, and Chef Maurice had put in calls to the head chefs of various neighbouring establishments with whom he had a passing acquaintance. None had heard of any white truffles being sold from local sources. All bemoaned the current economic climate and dearth of affordable truffles in general.

Which left him only one more call to make, which he would have to make in person. Chef Bonvivant, owner and executive chef at L'Epicure, had, according to his assistant, been unable to come to the telephone.

Given that they both had operated French restaurants in relatively close proximity for several decades, it was not surprising that Chef Maurice and Chef Bonvivant got on like a house on fire—that is to say, whenever they met, there was screaming, destruction of property, and sooner or later the need for large buckets of water.

"I cannot believe that Monsieur Ollie would sell to a . . . a . . . "

"Blaggard?" offered Arthur, who was familiar with the two chefs' past encounters.

"*Oui*, a blaggard like Bonvivant. Look at all this!" He waved a hand at the scenery outside, as they pulled up the long driveway past an immaculate rose garden and into a discreet paved courtyard at the back of the restaurant, full of Jaguars, Porsches and the occasional vintage coupé.

"If I were Ollie, Bonvivant would definitely be a good place to start offloading those truffles," said Arthur. "He's not exactly known to be tight with his chequebook."

"Bah. And look at what he spends it on." Chef Maurice gestured at the tall latticed windows at the back of the converted manor house and the valet rushing towards them to relieve them of the keys to Arthur's Aston Martin. "He spends more on tablecloths than he does on his ingredients."

"Really? I heard the lobster *thermidor* is rather g—" Arthur caught Chef Maurice's incensed stare. "Never mind."

Despite what his more naive customers might expect, Chef Gustave Bonvivant was not to be found in his kitchens. Instead, he was round the other side of the building, in a new glass-fronted annex which announced itself as: *The Bonvivant School of Culinary Excellence.*

"He dares to open a cooking school! That man, he could not even teach a dog to pi—"

"*Bonjour, messieurs!*" A glass door slid open to reveal Chef Bonvivant, resplendent in chef's whites, the creases ironed to razor sharpness. He was tall and slim, wore a neatly clipped beard, and, while Chef Maurice's accent seemed to grow stronger by the year, Chef Bonvivant's natural French tones had by now modulated their way into a catlike purr.

"So you have come to admire my new culinary school?" He bore down on them with every sign of self-satisfied pleasure. "Mr Wordington-Smythe, what an honour, I trust things are well at the England Observer? And Maurice, *mon cher collègue*, so kind of you to come visit. Come, let me take you on a tour."

He ushered them up the steps and past his assistant, who stood there attentively, clipboard poised.

"Alain, give us a few moments. I will call you when we are done." As his assistant scuttled off, he waved his arms at the room before them. "So what do you think?"

The room they stood in was about ten times the size of Le Cochon Rouge's kitchens. Rows of stainless steel hobs gleamed along each workstation, and the far wall was lined with the type of high-tech ovens that could not only roast a chicken, but probably then send it by email to your office.

"Bah, it is just a lot of kitchen toys," said Chef Maurice, eyeing the ovens with a hungry look. "It is a shame I see you have no students, though, Gustave."

"We're fully booked until next April," said Chef Bonvivant smoothly. "Today, we are closed because I am hosting a private masterclass for a special guest. You have heard of Karista? And her recent album *Dancing on Pins*?"

He looked at their blank faces. Chef Maurice refused to allow a radio in the kitchen, on the basis that Dorothy insisted on singing along, and Arthur's musical tastes generally verged on the Baroque.

"Ah, perhaps not." He wiped an invisible speck from a marbled work counter. "So, to what do I owe the pleasure of your visit?"

"We have come to speak to you about Monsieur Ollie Meadows."

"Ah, tragic, truly tragic. Of course, an establishment of our size has many suppliers, so we have been minimally affected, but I imagine his passing has been quite a blow to your little bistro?"

"Not at all. I have found an alternate supplier of the highest qualifications." Chef Maurice thought about Miss Fey's lab.

"Fantastic. I am most pleased to hear that. But what about Ollie did you wish to speak to me about?"

"We came to speak to you of truffles."

"Truffles?" Chef Bonvivant's face was a mask of polite non-chalance. "I wasn't aware that your menu stretched to truffles."

"I speak in particular of the truffles that Monsieur Ollie supplied you. White truffles, locally sourced, of a quality to rival the white truffles of Alba?"

"I see. I was not aware that Mr Meadows was dealing in those with anyone else."

"But of course he would come to me first," said Chef Maurice, radiating innocence. "We are of the same village.

But his stock was so plentiful, I told him he should try to sell the smaller truffles elsewhere."

"Indeed." Chef Bonvivant raised a sceptical eyebrow.

"May I ask how long Monsieur Ollie was supplying your kitchens with these new truffles?"

Chef Bonvivant glanced down at his watch. "Well, I cannot see what use it is to you. But he had been supplying these 'new truffles', as you call them, for three weeks prior to his disappearance."

"And he assured you he picked them himself, here locally?"

"The aroma was quite obvious, I felt. *Mon cher* Maurice, do not tell me you are planning to take up the truffle hunt yourself? Although, I can see that one has more free time in a village restaurant . . . "

"In fact, I am training a truffle pig of the highest calibre." Chef Maurice watched the other chef's face carefully, but he saw no sign of anything but mild disinterest.

"Very good," said Chef Bonvivant, inspecting his fingertips. "Though it may interest you to know that even Mr Meadows was not able to find the patch without assistance. At least that is what I understood, from under all his usual, ahem, braggadocio, shall we say."

"He actually admitted to stealing the patch from another forager?" said Arthur.

"Not according to him, though of course this was Mr Meadows speaking. No, he claimed someone had tipped him off."

"Why would anyone do that? It's like giving away the keys to the plantation—"

"To a particularly rapacious monkey, yes," said Chef Bonvivant. "I believe there was some question of settling a debt . . . " He looked down at his watch again. "I am afraid, gentlemen, that I will have to end our conversation here. Mademoiselle Karista should be arriving shortly."

As Chef Maurice and Arthur walked back to the car, a dark limousine pulled up in the yard and a raven-haired starlet swung her long legs out onto the path.

Chef Maurice stopped and bowed. "*Bonjour*, Mademoiselle Karista. You are here for a masterclass with Monsieur Bonvivant?"

"That I am," she drawled, adjusting her sunglasses.

"*Très bien*. You will find him in the glass building if you follow this path around here. One word of advice, *mademoiselle*. Be sure to address him as Monsieur Bon-Bon. He is most partial to that."

"That was a cruel and unusual punishment," said Arthur, as they drove away.

Chef Maurice didn't answer. He was thinking about what Chef Bonvivant had said.

It was dark outside and raining again.

Mrs Kristine Hart, of Grove Cottage, Farnley, opened her front door to the smell of lemons.

"*Bonsoir*, Madame Hart, we bring you lemon poppy seed cake," said the large red raincoat standing in the doorway.

"Oh. How kind . . . "

"We met the other night, you might remember, when the police found the car of Monsieur Ollie Meadows."

"I don't quite—"

"It was a trying time, I am sure, *madame*," said the sympathetic voice. "It is in fact about Monsieur Ollie, that we come to speak to you."

"Oh! Well, there's not much to tell you, Mr . . . ?"

"Please, call me Maurice. And this is Arthur, my—"

"Chauffeur, apparently."

"I told you, *mon ami*, I could come myself."

"After two glasses of cognac? Have you forgotten about the pheasant incident?"

"I was waiting for the lemon poppy seed cake to finish," said Chef Maurice, and handed Kristine the tinfoil-wrapped parcel, still warm from the oven. "And I became thirsty."

Mrs Hart looked back and forth between the two men. "Are you with the police?"

"There have been new developments in the case that we thought we should speak to you about, *madame*. Is Monsieur Hart also here?"

"He's in Amsterdam at the moment. What—"

"Perhaps it would be better if we spoke inside?"

"Oh, yes. Sorry, do come in."

She led them into the living room, where a stylish fake log fire was burning cheerily. The mantelpiece displayed several golfing trophies, a framed wedding photo of the couple—her in a trailing white lace dress, bouquet in hand, him in full morning suit, blond hair slicked back and white teeth flashing a smile—and a wilted vase of wild flowers.

"Ah, I see you still keep the flowers. As a token of remembrance, perhaps?"

Kristine's eyes narrowed. "I'm afraid I don't know what you mean."

"I think you do, *madame*. But do not worry, we will not speak to anyone. I assume that your husband did not know of your . . . friendship with Monsieur Ollie?"

Mrs Hart stared at them for a moment, then her eyes started to glisten. "No, he didn't. He doesn't. At least, he's never said a thing . . . we were in love, you know," she added suddenly. "Me and Ollie. Things had been bad with me and Nick for a long time, long before I even met Ollie."

Chef Maurice nodded understandingly, while privately impressed that there was enough love in the world left to make it go round, if so much was wasted on scoundrels like Ollie Meadows.

"You say that Monsieur Hart was unaware of your *affaire d'amour*. But there was a note found at Monsieur Ollie's cottage. It said something like: 'Keep away from things that don't belong to you. Or else.'"

Kristine's lips twisted. "That sounds like the kind of thing Nick would do. He likes threatening people. But wait . . . " Her knuckles tightened on her chair. "You're not saying you think Nick was involved in—"

"Monsieur Ollie's neighbour told us that a tall man with

blond hair visited Monsieur Ollie's cottage last Thursday, and that they had a loud argument."

"But Nick wouldn't— He was out of the country that weekend, I swear. He flew off Friday morning, I took him to the airport myself. And I— I saw Ollie that night. Nick couldn't have had anything to do with it. Swear on my life!"

"Did you ever go to the home of Monsieur Ollie?"

"No. He didn't want me visiting there, he said people would talk."

Chef Maurice thought about Mrs Eldridge and her binoculars. "I think he was right, *madame*. And when was the last time you saw Monsieur Ollie?"

Lipstick in the bathroom cabinet, he thought. Definitely a scallywag.

"That morning. The Saturday he . . . went missing. He went back home early in the morning, but he came back later and brought me these flowers"—she glanced with wet eyes at the mantelpiece—"then went up to the woods. And never came back. I went out looking for him, but . . . " She reached in her pockets for a tissue.

"Did Monsieur Ollie have his dog with him when he left?"

Kristine looked up. "Tufo? Yes, I'm pretty sure he did."

"Do you know for how long he had kept the dog?"

"Just a month or two, I think. Said he was looking after it for his uncle. He was kind like that. Do you know he called his mother in Italy, every day?"

"Quite an example, I am sure, *madame*," said Chef Maurice. "He did not say anything about this dog and some new, how do we say, line of business he was conducting? One that was perhaps quite lucrative?"

"I don't know much about his business. He didn't like to talk about it."

"Because of something illegal, perhaps? Like what they call the mushrooms *magique*?"

"Magic mushrooms?" said Kristine in surprise. "I asked Ollie about that once, but he said he didn't deal in them anymore, it wasn't worth the risk. No, in fact, I remember he was on about how his new venture was completely legal. Something top chefs would pay a fortune for, he said. He talked about how he'd dug himself up a pension."

Chef Maurice and Arthur exchanged looks.

"But he never showed you what he was selling?"

"No, I'm afraid not."

"And did he tell you how he came about such a venture?"

Kristine fingered the silver chain around her neck. "I got the feeling that someone had told him something they shouldn't have. He kept talking about someone giving away the family heirlooms. But, that's not to say it was easy. Whatever he had found, he worked hard for it," she added defensively. "He was doing a lot of research. He was down at the library at all hours."

"Do you know what for?" said Arthur.

"No idea. But he came round one day, pleased as a new

puppy. Gave me this." She lifted up the silver chain. "Gave me lots of things, the last few weeks," she sniffed.

They left Mrs Kristine Hart with her wilting petals and flowery memories.

"So it all comes back to the truffles," said Arthur. "Black gold, they say. Or white gold, in this case."

"'Top chefs'!" fumed Chef Maurice. "And he never offered them to me!"

"So what do we make of all this?" said Arthur, as they drove on past Farnley Woods.

"Hmmm, it is most interesting. I start to see a shape, under all that we find. The map that goes missing, the dog who runs away, the debts that must be paid— Wait, what is that on the side— Stop, stop the car!"

Chef Maurice tugged open the door and ran out into the road.

"Maurice, what the heck—"

But Chef Maurice was back in a moment, his scarf wrapped around what looked like a wet bundle of rags. The rags wriggled, and a little snout poked out and sniffed the air curiously.

It was Hamilton.

CHAPTER 19

The Welcome Back Hamilton party was set for the following evening. They hung up Le Cochon Rouge's 'Closed' sign, and any hungry visitors to the Cotswolds would have to find another village to stop off in for lunch.

Patrick was browning some beef ribs in preparation for several hours of slow braising, while Alf had been turned loose on the task of creating a sow nut pie, sow nut soup and sow nut trifle for the guest of honour.

Dorothy was at the kitchen table with a large pile of pink napkins, struggling to evolve an origami pig out of the stiff starched squares.

Patrick wandered over, tongs in hand. "Looks like a pink bomb," he offered.

"It's got a curly tail," said Dorothy, a tad defensively.

"It's funny how everyone thinks pigs are pink," said Alf. "Then you meet one, and they're a light brown, or black, or white with spots."

"I've never seen a bomb-shaped one, though."

"You just need a little more imagination, luv."

"Quite a bit more—"

Dorothy swiped at Patrick with a spare napkin. He jumped out of the way and went to check on his caramelising vegetables.

Arthur dropped by mid-morning, carrying an expensive-looking paper shopping bag—the type with the little string handles and dissolvable tissue paper wrapping, from the kind of store that assumes you'd never do something as crass as walk around in a downpour.

"Meryl sends her regards, via the medium of shopping." He pulled out a little knitted jumper, embroidered with the words: Little Porker.

"Ooooh, isn't that adorable," cooed Dorothy.

"Indeed," said Arthur. "So where's the pig of the moment?"

Patrick held back the temptation to ask 'which one?'— Chef Maurice having caused the sudden disappearance of their entire Stilton cheese stock overnight—and pointed to the backyard.

"Out in his field, happy as a pig in mud."

Arthur peered out of the window. Hamilton was running around his enclosure, squealing and leaping, while the two cows in the next-door field chewed their cud and watched this display with mild interest.

"Is he okay?"

"He's been like that all morning. Happy to be out in the fresh air, I guess, after being cooped up who knows where."

"All fit and present then?"

"Well, the vet came round first thing this morning, said he couldn't see anything to worry about. He's lost a little weight, but I think he'll put it back on pretty soon." Patrick nodded towards Alf, who was sorting sow nuts by size for his trifle.

"No doubt. So where's Maurice got to today?"

"Funny you should say that, luv," said Dorothy, who'd now moved on to pink swans. "We've not seen him all morning."

Arthur groaned. "That cannot be a good thing."

Despite the appearance of mindless gallivanting, Hamilton was in fact in the middle of a serious re-enactment of his imprisonment for the benefit of his enthralled bovine audience, who found the whole thing fascinating.

There was shock (a pignapping!), torture (or at least, a serious lack of apples), a heroic escape, and finally a most fortuitous ending, being reunited with his owner as he trudged his way back home.

It was, all in all, a cut above the usual stories the cows heard down at the milking parlour, though occasionally one of the sheep turned up with a pretty good yarn.

They were particularly interested in the identity of Hamilton's pignapper. (Cows being, by nature, very law-abiding creatures, they were looking forward to getting some righteous stampeding done should they come across the pignapper in future.)

But that question was easily enough answered. All you had to do, according to Hamilton, was look for the human with the big piggy-bite mark on their arm.

Chef Maurice was also having a busy morning.

Come daybreak, he spent a good hour stomping up and down the fields behind Ollie's cottage, prodding at the dewy grass with a long stick. Eventually, he found what he was looking for.

Next, he drove over to Oxford to pay a visit to the University Department of Plant Pathology and received a guided tour from the gratified but rather puzzled Deputy Head of Department.

On his way back to Beakley, he stopped at Laithwaites Manor to invite Brenda to Hamilton's homecoming party and to twist her arm for her walnut-and-coffee-bean cake recipe, which she scribbled down after extracting a promise that it would not turn up on the restaurant's menu.

Rejuvenated by a large cup of tea with four sugars, he headed for the Beakley library and sweet-talked the librarian into letting him down into the archives by means of a tray of caramel fudge brownies.

One dusty hour later, he was on the move again, this time to see a pheasant broker over near Cowton, who bought pheasants from local landowners and game-shooting companies to sell to the high-end restaurants and gastropubs, where people were apparently willing to pay a premium to pick lead shot out of their teeth after dinner.

He also popped into the Cowton police station to see PC Lucy, who, after being located hiding under her desk, rolled her eyes at his suggestion, reluctantly agreed to see what she could do, and promised to be at Le Cochon Rouge in time for Hamilton's dinnertime celebrations.

He paid one final special visit in Beakley, where a large bottle of fine cognac may or may not have changed hands.

Thus prepared, he motored back to the restaurant. He really hoped it was all going to work. Because if things went wrong, there was a chance he'd end up with something a lot more deadly than pie on his face.

Dusk fell on the kitchens at Le Cochon Rouge.

"Maurice?"

"*Oui?*"

"This seating plan of yours." Arthur waved the piece of paper. "What exactly are you up to?"

"Ah, you think I should have sat the gentlemen alternately with the ladies? To be more traditional?"

Arthur looked at the diagram again. Indeed, Brenda was sat next to Miss Fey, while on the other side of the table, PC Lucy would be tasked with making small talk with Mrs Eldridge.

"And who's this Peter?"

"He is the son of Madame Laithwaites. He was there when I visited. I thought it would be rude to not invite him."

"Even so, we're still a bit short on men. But anyway, that wasn't what I was talking about. You're up to something. I can tell."

Chef Maurice looked up from tasting the jus for the beef ribs. "I have no idea what you mean."

"Meryl says she saw you down at the library today. What's that all about?"

"I thought I should start to take an interest in the plants of this region." Chef Maurice pointed to a battered copy of *Egbert's Miscellany of Wild Botany* sitting on the counter.

"You're not planning on some course of rash action, are you?"

"*Quelle idée!* This a simple dinner of celebration, to welcome back *mon* Hamilton. And do not worry, should there be misbehaving, there will be a police lady in attendance."

He winked and nudged Patrick, who almost dropped the tray of beef ribs.

"I think I'll be staying in the kitchen, chef, if it's all the same to you."

"Bah! One unreturned phone call, and you are in retreat? You must go for the chase!"

Arthur wasn't so sure. He was all for gentlemanly persistence, of course, but when your intended was a member of the police force, perhaps you had to tread a little more carefully . . .

"I'm not retreating, chef, I'm just giving her some space. I'm sure she's still busy with Ollie's murder case."

"Ah, then do not be despondent. The case may be closed sooner than you think."

"There, I knew it, you *are* up to something!" Arthur put his fingers to his temples. "Maurice, how many times do I have to tell you not to—"

Arthur was saved from adding to the count by the arrival of their guests, who'd all turned up at the front door with unnerving punctuality.

Mrs Eldridge was already engaged in deep conversation with Brenda about the local traffic situation. Miss Fey, wearing a smart dress but no lab coat, was exchanging pleasantries with Peter Laithwaites regarding his future academic plans. The young man stood there, slouched with hands in pockets. He had, Arthur noted, a particularly annoying laugh, like a small hyena stuck down a hole.

PC Lucy handed a paper bag to Chef Maurice. "Just a little something for Hamilton."

Inside, was a pile of assorted apples and a brand-new bobble hat.

"You are too kind, *mademoiselle*. And about the other thing . . . ?"

PC Lucy lowered her voice. "It all checked out. But I still don't see—"

"You will see in time. Very soon, in fact. But first we eat."

He turned to his group of guests.

"*Alors*, now that everyone is here, please come, sit!"

Chef Maurice took his place at the head of the long table that had been set up in the middle of the dining room. Hamilton sat in a child's highchair at his elbow, and Arthur took his place on Chef Maurice's right. Opposite Arthur sat Miss Fey, then Brenda and her son, Peter. On Arthur's right was PC Lucy, then Mrs Eldridge.

The eighth place, at the other end of the table, was laid with crockery but empty. Arthur consulted the seating plan; the last box was blank. He gave Chef Maurice a questioning look.

"Ah!" said Chef Maurice, raising a finger. "You will see in good time. Now, *bon appétit!*"

As if on cue, Dorothy appeared bearing a giant mushroom tart, the top covered in golden flaky pastry, steaming with the aromas of garlic and thyme.

Hamilton's sow nut tartlet was placed on an enamel plate in front of him and disappeared within seconds.

Chef Maurice raised his glass. "Madame Fey, I offer congratulations on the superb quality of your produce, and thank you for sending these fine *champignons* with such speed."

"My pleasure, Mr Manchot. Always a delight to see my work go to such good use."

The wine, a white from Bordeaux, was flowing easily. Conversation turned to the antics of local politicians, the state of young people's education, and remembrances of other fine bottles of wine. Arthur found himself starting to relax. He wondered if it would be untoward to help himself to the last slice of mushroom tart.

Chef Maurice tapped his fork on his wineglass, and an expectant silence fell over the table, punctuated only by a clatter of enamel as Hamilton upended his empty plate onto the floor, on the off chance that another sow nut tart was lurking beneath.

"My friends, I have a confession. It is not just for the celebration of Hamilton's return that I make this invitation."

He cleared his throat.

"It is, I am afraid, about the murder of Monsieur Ollie Meadows that we sit here now."

Arthur let out a small groan.

"Because I can tell you that, tonight, his murderer is sitting with us. Here at this table."

Six faces (and one snout) turned to him in amazement and incredulity.

At this point Dorothy bustled out of the kitchen, oven gloves on her hands.

"Ready for the main course? What are you all sitting around here like pumpkins for?"

They looked at her.

She put her gloved hands on hips.

"Well? And who's going to finish this last slice of mushroom pie?"

CHAPTER 20

Once Dorothy had come and gone with the big casserole of beef rib stew, tut-tutting at their lack of party spirit, Chef Maurice cleared his throat once more.

"Throughout the search for the murderer of Monsieur Ollie, it seemed that always there was the question of money. Money found in Monsieur Ollie's house, money to borrow a dog, money for illegal mushrooms. And most valuable of all, money for these."

He pulled a large white truffle out of his pocket. Hamilton gave a squeal and tried to stand up in his highchair to reach it.

"A few evenings ago, an intruder broke into Monsieur Ollie's cottage. What did the intruder take? Just a map, an old map of the area including Farnley Woods. A map much reproduced, and so of little value.

"And what did he not take? There was much money hidden in Monsieur Ollie's house, and there also a bag of these." He raised the truffle. "This is a white truffle, much the same as the very expensive, very desirable white truffle of Alba, apart from a small difference in the *arôme*, only detectable to the most delicate of senses."

Arthur rolled his eyes.

"But to senses like these," continued Chef Maurice, "it was undoubtable that these were white *English* truffles, never seen before. And so very rare and very valuable, even more so than the white truffle of Alba."

"Looks like a potato," whispered Mrs Eldridge to PC Lucy.

"Shh. It's a mushroom. Or a type of fungi, I think."

"Doesn't look very fun to me."

"Ahem," said Chef Maurice, glaring at them. "So we ask ourselves, why did the thief not steal these too? Perhaps he could not find them. Perhaps he was"—he coughed—"interrupted. Perhaps we will never know. But the finding of these new truffles can be no coincidence when we consider also the disappearance of Monsieur Ollie. So I go to search out these truffles, in the hope to discover where we might find Monsieur Ollie too."

"Actually—" began Arthur, but Chef Maurice hurriedly cut him off.

"*Therefore*, I sought to find myself a pig who could be trained to be a truffle pig—"

"*Actually*, you started out looking for a d—"

"Shhh, *pas devant le cochon!*" hissed Chef Maurice, looking in alarm at Hamilton.

The rest of the table looked at each other.

"So," said Chef Maurice, recovering his thread of thought, "we take Hamilton to walk in the woods of Farnley. But we do not find truffles. Instead, we find Monsieur Ollie. He has been shot, and his body dragged and hidden.

"So it seems, the hunt for truffles is a very dangerous thing. But we continue, in all cases! And like this, we come to be noticed by someone. Someone who is not happy that we search for truffles, like Monsieur Ollie did. And so they threaten. They steal Hamilton, right in the home of *chère* Madame Laithwaites here."

Brenda gave a small shudder.

"So it is clear, we are not the only people to know about the new truffle. They send a note, telling me to stay away from their business. But we do not stop. We ask questions, to those who knew Monsieur Ollie. And so it is we hear, Monsieur Ollie did not find the truffle patch by accident. He knew, at the very least, of its existence. So he sought to find it, and we know he was successful. But then he paid a price.

"So we must ask ourselves, who did the truffle patch belong to? Who knew of its existence before Monsieur Ollie? These are large truffles, mature truffles. The trees producing these truffles must have been in production for many years before this. Did they stay under the ground, silent? Or did somebody know about them, and has been profiting for all this time? And when Monsieur Ollie stole into their patch, did this person look to stop him?

"So I also must go in search of this person. Now, it is clear that this person must know much of truffles and how to discover them. But the searching of truffles is not an easy task. One must have knowledge of the woods, and a knowledge of truffles. And this person must have a desperation for money, enough that they would kill to stop Monsieur Ollie."

"Well, that's easy," said Mrs Eldridge triumphantly. "It's that so-called uncle of his. I heard talk that he's a truffle hunter, along with that scruffy little dog. Saw him take off in his car earlier, hasn't been back since. On the run, I expect, right after you came and had that big argy-bargy with him this morning, Mr Maurice. You better get moving, dear, if you want to catch him." This last bit was to PC Lucy, whom she poked in the leg with her cane.

"*Non, non*, Madame Eldridge. I am not talking of Monsieur Mannozzi. While at first I did have suspicions and alerted the police—"

"Which I'm still getting flack for, by the way," muttered PC Lucy.

"—it would not make sense. How would Monsieur Mannozzi know of a truffle patch in an area of the country far from where he lives? And even if he did, why would he then agree to lend his nephew his valuable truffle dog?

"*Non*, it is not Monsieur Mannozzi who we must consider. But there is another expert of the woods. One with a hidden interest in truffles.

"I speak, of course, of Madame Fey."

Miss Fey did not move, apart from raising her eyebrows.

"Is that so?" she said calmly.

"Today, *madame*, I make a visit to your university department. It was most informative. You claimed little interest in truffles when we first met you, yet your current work concerns the cultivation of the truffle fungus, including the white truffle of Alba."

"But that's impossible," said Arthur. "No one's managed it. It's why we pay a fortune for those things!"

"But perhaps someone with enough knowledge has managed it," said Chef Maurice, watching Miss Fey. "The gentleman at the university also gave mention of another thing. That the laboratory of Madame Fey was under threat to close, because of a sudden lack of funds. And where had these funds been coming from? A hidden truffle patch, perhaps, cultivated by Madame Fey herself? And recently depleted due to the actions of Monsieur Ollie?"

Miss Fey regarded Chef Maurice with an amused expression. "I think, Mr Manchot, that you misunderstand the cut and thrust of the world of academic funding. All labs are perpetually underfunded. We do not go around killing people off because of it. And if I had indeed cultivated the white Alba truffle—on English soils, no less—it would be my scientific duty to make my research known. Though I must thank you for bringing these truffles to my attention. You can be assured that our lab will be looking into this with great scrutiny."

She smiled. "And of course, I assume you have absolutely no actual evidence to suggest I would do something as ridiculous as to shoot Ollie Meadows in cold blood?"

Arthur held his breath. What had Chef Maurice been up to this morning? And what had he found? Had he really—

"*Non, madame*, you are correct. I have no evidence." Chef Maurice sat back down, looking deflated. Then he smiled. "You are also correct that you would not do something as ridiculous as to shoot Monsieur Ollie. But not because you would not stop in the removal of a rival, if there was such. But in this case, to shoot him like so would be most *unintelligent*. In the woods, not far from a main road and houses? *Impossible!*

"I suspect, Madame Fey, if you committed a crime, it would be one of much better planning and execution. But, *non*, I do not think you are responsible for the murder of Monsieur Ollie."

He gave her a wink.

"But you are not the only one at this table who was in acquaintance with Monsieur Ollie." He looked around at his guests. "Mademoiselle Lucy, of course, dealt with Monsieur Ollie at times when he was caught in minor crimes. Madame Eldridge, too, knew Ollie well as his neighbour, and knew much of his dealings, how he comes and goes."

Mrs Eldridge leaned over to PC Lucy. "Is that right? Is he accusing me of being the murderer?"

"Shhh, I'm sure he's not." PC Lucy looked up. "You're not, are you, Maurice?"

"*Un moment, mademoiselle*. We then have Madame Laithwaites here—"

"I've never even set eyes on the man!" said Brenda, more bewildered than indignant.

"Ah, you may have not, Madame Brenda, but if I am right, your son sitting beside you knew Monsieur Ollie very well indeed."

Peter Laithwaites, who'd been sitting in sullen silence, looked up suddenly.

"Wha—"

"Am I right in thinking, Monsieur Peter, that you and your friends, who delight in meeting in Cowton public houses such as The Office, were in the habit of purchasing highly illegal mushrooms from Monsieur Ollie?"

Arthur gasped. "I *knew* I recognised his voice from somewhere."

Brenda was staring open-mouthed at her son.

"Peter James Laithwaites—"

"And perhaps you ended up owing Monsieur Ollie quite a large sum of money. Which he demanded from you."

"And which I paid back!" said Peter, managing to unfreeze his tongue. "I had nothing against Ollie, I swear, the shooting has nothing to do with me. I was in Ibiza, you can check the flight records—"

"Which we have," said Chef Maurice, with a nod at PC Lucy.

"—and so you'll see, I wasn't even in the country the day he was shot!"

"And how," replied Chef Maurice triumphantly, "do you know *the exact day that Monsieur Ollie was shot?*"

Peter's face was transformed into a look of horror.

"And then there is the map that you stole. *Regarde*, Arthur, Monsieur Peter fits the description of the intruder who you observed entering Monsieur Ollie's cottage on the Monday night."

Arthur looked Peter up and down. "Well, he does. But I still don't see why—"

"Aha, there is the question. Why would Peter steal the map, on which we presume Monsieur Ollie marked the patch of truffles? How would this young man know about the truffles and the map, in order to steal it?

"So today, I took a walk around the fields behind Monsieur Ollie's cottage. And I found this."

He extracted from under the table a crumpled, slightly soggy mass of paper, now welded solid by recent rains. The faint traces of roads and land markings were barely recognisable on the scrap facing upwards.

"*Mesdames et messieurs*, what we have here is most likely the map that was stolen from Monsieur Ollie. But what was it doing in a field, in complete ruin? Even if the intruder had dropped it, why not go back and pick it? Could they be in such a hurry?

"Then I realised, my logic, it was all upside down. What if the intruder, the young Monsieur Peter here, was not seeking to steal the map, but to destroy it?

"What if, in fact, Monsieur Peter was not in search of the truffle ground, but instead was the one who had *told* Monsieur Ollie of the existence of the Farnley Wood truffles?"

He turned to the stunned young man.

"You say that you paid Monsieur Ollie back, but it was not in money, *n'est-ce pas?* It was, I think, in truffles. But Monsieur Ollie, he was a greedy man. He was not happy with a truffle or two. He wanted the source, which you would not tell him. But he knew the woods well, and he went in search of it. And, unfortunately for him, he found it."

Peter turned to his mother.

"Mum—"

"No." Brenda's face was grey. "Let him finish his nonsense. He obviously has no proof, else why sit here spouting all this . . . this . . . " Her voice faltered as she looked across the table at PC Lucy, who was staring at Peter.

"But Mum—"

"I won't have anyone saying you ran out of here like a criminal! Tomorrow, we'll . . . we'll get you a lawyer . . . "

"A wise decision, *madame*," said Chef Maurice.

"But I don't understand," said Arthur. "How would Peter here—clearly not the most outdoorsy of fellows, I'm afraid—know anything about finding truffles in the first place? Truffles that not even someone like Ollie knew were there?"

"Aha!" Chef Maurice eyes lit up. "This is another thing I discover this morning. The reason that Monsieur Peter Laithwaites knows that the truffles were in Farnley Woods is because it was the Laithwaites who planted them there in the first place."

"Wait a moment, old chap," said Arthur after a moment's silence, "you just don't go around planting truffles. Believe me, I've tried."

(That was a few years ago, and Meryl had been less than impressed to find her favourite rose bush half dug up, and her inebriated husband attempting to plant the remains of a truffle soufflé in its spot.)

Chef Maurice turned to Miss Fey.

"This is, of course, your area of knowledge, *madame*."

"You'd need trees, young ones, with roots inoculated with the correct truffle spore," said Miss Fey promptly. "It's been done with the lesser varieties, even with the black Périgord, but I've never seen a successful case of the white Alba."

"But I've heard it takes decades for the truffles to fruit!" said Arthur. "How would Peter—"

"Ah, but I suspect it was not Monsieur Peter, but his *grand-père*, Monsieur Archibald Laithwaites, who was a great gardener and lover of plants, who planted the truffle trees. Most likely from a variety of oak already growing in Farnley Woods."

"Rubbish," muttered Peter.

"Ah, you think so? Then you must see this."

Chef Maurice reached under the table and pulled up a sheaf of large photocopies. "These are from the library. They show the same area in different years, the same type of maps that Madame Brenda was kind enough to show

217

us. The librarian informed me that Monsieur Ollie too had been looking at these maps. And he took a copy of the map from 1957. Why that year?"

Chef Maurice shuffled the sheets. "If we regard the Laithwaites Manor estate today, we see there are no areas of trees big enough to be a truffle planting. But Madame Brenda told us her father was forced to sell areas of land to pay his debts. And this was in 1961."

Chef Maurice laid the two maps, the old and current, side-by-side. Mrs Eldridge struggled to her feet to get a better look.

"*Regarde*, the areas of land that made part of the Laithwaites estate in 1957. And today, they are not there. This one, in particular"—he jabbed a finger at the map—"was a large area of tree land."

"Why," said Brenda icily, "would my father sell off an area of land that he knew was producing truffles?"

"But they would not have shown by then. We go back ten years"—Chef Maurice brought out a map of 1948—"there were no woods marked there. By the time your father had necessity to sell the land, perhaps he was thinking his experiment had failed. Only after many years, he discovered his success. And passed this knowledge to his family, of course."

"This is all complete nonsense!" said Brenda. "I don't know when exactly this Ollie was shot, but Peter is telling the truth. He only arrived back on the Monday, records will show this."

"Yes, they will, *madame*," said Chef Maurice softly. "In fact, Mademoiselle Lucy has already checked them, and Monsieur Peter arrived back, as you say, on the Monday afternoon. So he could not have been in Farnley Woods the Saturday before, when Monsieur Ollie went missing."

"Well, there you are, then!"

"*But*, Madame Brenda, when we come to visit you on the Thursday, the day Hamilton is taken from your kitchen, you tell us your son is arriving back that evening. The *Thursday* evening. Why do you lie?

"And so the truth, it comes out. Monsieur Peter, yes, was not in the country on Saturday, but you, Madame Brenda, *you were*.

"We talked about the truffles, but how would the son know of the truffles, and the mother would not? It is not believable. *You* are the one who has looked after the truffle patch from the time your father told you of it. *You* were in the woods on Saturday, when you found Monsieur Ollie picking truffles on the ground you considered your own, considered part of your estate. You were there, and you shot him, and dragged his body away from the patch. When Monsieur Peter arrives back on Monday, you send him out to make sure there is nothing in Monsieur Ollie's cottage that could link your family to the crime."

"Absolutely preposterous!" cried Brenda. She leapt up, dragging Peter to his feet beside her, and marched towards the door. "I will not listen any more to your . . . your

219

inflammatory stories and half-baked ideas. You have no shred of proof, not a single—"

She reached for the door, but it flew back inwards before she could touch it.

A huge figure loomed in the doorway. It grinned at her.

CHAPTER 21

It was Luciano, carrying a large sack.

He strode past Brenda without a glance and upended the sack onto the table. A dozen large white truffles rolled out.

"Just where you said they'd be, Signor Maurice," he said cheerfully. "Tufo and I, we had a very good time. And these truffles, they are something special, I can tell you tha—"

It was at this point that Brenda lost it. She grabbed up a poker from near the fire and ran towards Luciano.

"Thieving scoundrel! Those truffles belong to the Laithwaites family! I'll kill you, just like I killed that scum of a nephew of yours. Thieves, the lot of you!"

"I think," murmured Arthur to Chef Maurice, as they watched Luciano duck and shield himself with a meaty arm and PC Lucy jump up to grab Brenda from behind, "that we might just be able to count that as a confession."

It was some time later. Brenda Laithwaites had been taken down to the Cowton police station, still screaming obscenities,

221

with Peter following miserably. PC Lucy, who'd had a tape recorder running the whole time, told Arthur she'd have to see how things went but it seemed as good an admission of guilt as they'd probably ever get.

Luciano had taken his place at the far end of the table, and Alf and Patrick had finished their kitchen duties and had taken the seats of their recently departed guests. Dorothy had rushed off down into the village with a sudden batch of 'errands to run'.

"So when did you figure out it was Brenda all along?" asked Arthur, tucking into a long-neglected plate of beef ribs.

"Ah, *mon ami*, I tell you, it was from the very beginning when we met in the woods. The way she talked as if she owned the land—"

"Codswallop. I don't believe you."

Chef Maurice deflated a little. "Perhaps not. But from the moment of Hamilton's disappearance, I had suspicions about this lady. She told us of a masked gunman bursting into her kitchen—so much drama, so much theatre. It did not seem real. And it wasn't!"

"She made the whole thing up?" said Patrick.

"I think not, but I think she arranged it all. Peter had returned earlier in the week. He would burst in and take Hamilton, while she destroyed a very handsome teapot and screamed most loudly. Remember, she was most insistent that the intruder was very big, very bulky—the complete opposite of her son."

"But I still don't see how—" began Arthur.

"Aha." Chef Maurice leant back in his chair, resting his hands comfortably on his stomach. "I just begin. It was not, I make the confession, until yesterday that my thoughts turned completely to the Laithwaites. But Madame Hart, she told us something about Monsieur Ollie stealing 'family heirlooms'. And I remember how Madame Brenda talked, as if the woods still belonged to her family.

"So then I make my enquiries. Madame Brenda tells us she is not a fan of shooting. Yet Monsieur Brooks, the pheasant broker, tells me Madame Brenda brings to him several dozen pheasants each October. She is, says Monsieur Brooks, a most excellent shot. And then I ask Monsieur Luciano here to ask questions into the sale of mysterious English truffles in this country, as he has many contacts in the sale of truffles."

Luciano grunted, mouth full of beef rib, and saluted Chef Maurice.

"It was inconceivable that Madame Brenda was not selling the truffles for profit. And yet, she could not be selling locally, as we would know already. And so it was. After many phone calls, Luciano finds a dealer of truffles near York who claims a supply of unusual white truffles, from 'an English lady from the south'. He refused to give a name, but said that the lady would travel up every week in truffle season, with a grey poodle. *Et voilà!*"

Arthur set down his fork, plate empty. A thought had just occurred to him. "So that note we found at Ollie's cottage—not the one from Luciano—but the other one, about staying away from their property. All this time we assumed it was, ahem, an irate husband but—"

"*Oui*, it was Madame Brenda. Today, I go and ask her to write a recipe for walnut-and-coffee-bean cake—a most excellent cake, though perhaps I would add a little coffee liqueur . . . " He drifted off for a moment, contemplating this.

"Maurice!"

"Eh? Oh, yes, so I brought this to Mademoiselle Lucy, and we compared to that note. They are written by the same hand."

"Cor!" said Alf, who'd been listening with eyes wide as saucepans. "And then you got Mr Manozzy here"—Alf looked over at their last guest, who, napkin tucked into shirt, was demolishing an extra-large truffle-covered omelette with great concentration, while Tufo sat at his feet, licking a beef bone—"to go up to the woods and find those truffles, so that Mrs Laithwaites would get all mad and riled up and attack him with a poker. Genius!"

Chef Maurice nodded. "But of course," he said modestly.

"So it wasn't just to make sure you got a batch of truffles out of there before the police crawled all over the site?" said Arthur, raising an eyebrow.

"*Mon ami*, I am hurt!"

"But well-provisioned, I'm sure."

"What a lot of fuss over a pile of mushrooms," said Mrs Eldridge, who was also sampling a freshly made truffle omelette. "They ain't bad, I'll give you that, but they don't taste of much, do they? Not a patch on a good old chestnut mushroom."

They stared at her.

"What?" she said defensively. "They ain't."

CHAPTER 22

It was now November. The trees had shaken off their leaves, and the weather was coasting inexorably into the blustery winter blues.

Hamilton had settled happily into his field behind Le Cochon Rouge, snug in his little cocoon of hay as the wind huffed and puffed outside. The cows, feeling starved of excitement, were currently loitering down the other end of their field, right by the main road, in case anyone felt like cownapping them.

Miss Fey, thanks to the joint publicity from Arthur's article and her soon-to-be-groundbreaking research into white Alba truffle cultivation, had expanded her mushroom business to the point where she was now able to take on a lab-assistant-cum-apprentice-forager, a nervous young woman who lived in constant fear that her employer would poison her if she broke a single pipette.

Luciano had gone off to Italy with Tufo to make the most of the Alba truffle season. He promised to return next autumn to train Hamilton into a champion truffle pig.

In the kitchens of Le Cochon Rouge, November was a welcome respite before the frantic Christmas season. Alf's new foraging skills had brought in a glut of hawthorn berries and, today, head chef, sous-chef and commis were all covered head to toe in sticky red jam as they bottled up enough jars to accompany the cheeseboard through the winter.

There was a knock on the back door and PC Lucy stuck her head round.

"I tried to phone, but no one picked up, so I thought I'd just walk over." She looked them up and down. "Is this a bad time?"

"But of course not," said Chef Maurice. "It is a delight to see you, *mademoiselle*. It has been too long."

"Yes, sorry about that. The Meadows case has been keeping everyone pretty busy, but it's now wrapping up."

"Madame Brenda, she has been found guilty?"

"The trial's not till next month, but she's already confessed to everything. She tried to keep Peter out of it, so I think he'll get off with minor charges."

"Hmph, pig stealer," muttered Chef Maurice. "And what will happen to the Manor?"

"I hear she's had to sell it. To pay the legal fees."

"Ah, a shame. I sometimes wonder if the *grand-père* Laithwaites had perhaps planted more truffle trees within—"

"Don't you even *think* of trespassing on that land."

"But of course not. Please, come in. A coffee, perhaps, or a *chocolat chaud*?"

PC Lucy hesitated by the door. "Actually, I was hoping to have a word with Patrick . . . "

Chef Maurice prodded Patrick forwards with a jammy spoon. "*Voilà*, he is all yours."

"Um." Patrick's face was red as a hawthorn berry. "Shall we go outside?"

They went out into the backyard, while Chef Maurice and Alf shuffled themselves over to a window to watch the proceedings. To their disappointment, Patrick led PC Lucy around the corner of the building, out of their line of sight.

They appeared some minutes later. There was a smear of red jam on PC Lucy's cheek, and Patrick wore a big dreamy grin.

"Do you think that counts as assaulting a police officer?" asked Alf.

Chef Maurice stroked his moustache. "I think probably not."

"Shame."

PC Lucy waved goodbye to them from the gate, and shouted promises to come over to try the new Christmas lunch menu.

Patrick spent the rest of the afternoon in a happy daze.

Like truffles, sometimes things just need a little time to grow.

J.A. Lang is a British mystery author. She lives in Oxford, England, with her husband, an excessive number of cookbooks, and a sourdough starter named Bob.

Want more Chef Maurice?

To receive email notification when the next Chef Maurice mystery is released, as well as news about future book releases by J.A. Lang, subscribe to the newsletter at:

www.jalang.net/newsletter

Bruce County Public Library
1243 Mackenzie Rd.
Port Elgin ON N0H 2C6

CPSIA information can be obtained at www.ICGtesting.com
Printed in the USA
LVOW11s0512200516

489059LV00003B/179/P